P9-ASN-800

The
Half Child

KATHLEEN HERSOM

SIMON & SCHUSTER BOOKS FOR YOUNG READERS
Published by Simon & Schuster
New York • London • Toronto • Sydney • Tokyo • Singapore

Author's Note

The Half Child is set in very real places, reaching from Weardale in County Durham to Swaledale in Yorkshire, between 1644 and 1700, but a few local details are invented, as are all the main characters, and any resemblance to living persons (or their ancestors) is entirely accidental.

SIMON & SCHUSTER BOOKS FOR YOUNG READERS
Simon & Schuster Building, Rockefeller Center
1230 Avenue of the Americas, New York, New York 10020
Copyright © 1989 by Kathleen Hersom
All rights reserved including the right of reproduction in whole or in part in any form.
Originally published in Great Britain by Simon & Schuster Limited. First U.S. edition 1991.
SIMON & SCHUSTER BOOKS FOR YOUNG READERS
is a trademark of Simon & Schuster.
Manufactured in the United States of America

10   9   8   7   6   5   4   3   2   1

Library of Congress Cataloging-in-Publication Data
Hersom, Kathleen. The half child / Kathleen Hersom.   p.   cm.   Summary: In seventeenth-century
Yorkshire, Lucy's younger sister Sarah is suspected by many to be a changeling, a fairy child substituted by the
fairies for a human child. [1. Sisters—Fiction.   2. Superstition—Fiction.   3. Yorkshire (England)—
Fiction.]   I. Title.   PZ7.H43243Hal   1991   [Fic]—dc20   90-24079   CIP   AC

ISBN 0-671-74225-6

The
Half Child

*With gratitude to all my young friends from
Earl's House Hospital, Durham,
wherever they may be now*

Contents

But I, so wild,
Your disgrace, with the queer brown face, was never,
Never, I know, but half your child!

Charlotte Mew, *The Changeling*

1

Our Sarah

It is cuckoo time in the year of our Lord 1700.

I, Lucy Watson, am sitting at the old trestle table in that same cottage in Wulsingham in Weredale where my sister Sarah was born fifty-five years ago, six years after me. Although I am not a very good scholar, I am trying to write down the story of us Emersons, particularly Sarah—Emerson being my name before I married Henry.

Sarah did not talk as plainly as other children. She had a growling voice, so that most people could not understand what she was saying. They did not think she would be saying anything that mattered anyway, so they never listened carefully to the rumbling sounds that stumbled out of her mouth. They were sure, too, that that was the way changelings always spoke, slurring the words together and leaving words out, and as they had never had the chance to learn fairy language themselves, they just shrugged their shoulders and paid no more heed.

But I was right beside her through long days, and

nights too, listening to what she was telling me, and trying to give her what she wanted. So I learned to guess
fairly well what she meant—much better than our
mother or father could.

I mind well the night our Sarah was born. It was the
dark time of the year with a hard, black frost.

Mother was big, very big because of Sarah, and lying
alone on the great bed where she always slept with
Father. Father was up, pottering about. We children
slept in the loft chamber, same as they did, but on little
pallet beds in the corners. Richard had one to himself,
and his twin sister, Martha, and me were together on
another. Granny slept below on the settle by the kitchen
fire because her doddery old legs would not take her up
the ladder into the loft. Tall, bony and full of corners she
was.

I had been wakened by Father tapping with his ham-
mer on the fireback to rouse Mistress Charlton, who
lived in the cottage next to ours. As soon as she came in
he took his lanthorn and went to fetch Janey Foster, the
Wise Woman from the Upper End. No sooner had he
gone than Mistress Charlton started rushing about the
loft like a hen on a hot griddle.

"Out of here! Out of here, you bairns! No room for
you with the babby coming any minute now!" she cack-
led, flapping her cape at us to shoo us down the ladder
out of her way, but into the way of Granny, who was
twittering and grumbling at being disturbed so long
before dawn by our shuffling and whispering.

When Granny had herself properly awake and finished with complaining, she started trying to order everything that was going on above, even after Janey Foster was there. It was plain that it rankled with her that she could not be up in the loft herself to see what was being done and what was not being done, blaming and correcting and disapproving right in the center of it all, instead of standing there at the bottom of the ladder shouting up at them.

". . . And there are cloths in the big press in the corner, there'll be plenty hot water down here. Martha can bring it up in the great jug when 'tis needed. Have you the cradle all ready? Mind you do not set it rocking till the babby is safe inside it. There's ill luck in rocking an empty cradle. . . . Do you hear me, Mistress Charlton? . . . And the candle . . . you had best light it now for fear of forgetting it later. There must be a candle kept burning always, against stealing by the Little People."

She kept on saying that about the candle. No one answered her. I expect they were far too busy doing things the way they wanted to do them to listen to her.

Then at last we heard a baby hullabaloo, and Mistress Charlton was calling down to us that it was a girl babby that had been born, "neither too little nor too big, and the bairns can come and have a keek at her in a little while." So, in a little while, we did. And there was Sarah looking tiny and red and twisted and wrinkled and very, very cross, much crosser than I had ever seen her at any time since.

Our mother said, "She is beautiful!" which might seem a strange thing to say of a babby with a humped back such as Sarah had, but Mistress Charlton and Janey Foster gave no opinion, and I noticed that they kept their eyes and noses turned away from Sarah as they busied about, as though she were tainted meat. I didn't think our Richard and our Martha cared very much for her. I did not think she was beautiful either, only ugly in her own special kind of way that was different from other babbies. I loved her, all the same, from the first moment I saw her.

Then old Granny was back at the foot of the ladder again.

"I shall want to see the bairn presently, mind!" she shouted. "But before you bring her down here you must stand up on a stool, or on the bed or summat with her, do you hear that, Janey Foster? Mistress Charlton can do that for you if you are busy with our Margaret, but it *must* be done! Do you hear me, Janey? Ill fortune always follows when a newly born is taken down afore it is taken up. You should know that, Janey Foster!"

I could tell that Janey Foster was vexed at being told her business, for hadn't she been a Wise Woman for as long as most could remember, and if anyone knew about taking newborns up before they were taken down, and the way to guard against thieving by the Little People, wouldn't it be her?

When we were back in the kitchen again, Richard said he thought the babby was an ugly little devil.

"But Mother said she was beautiful," I told him.

Martha laughed. "That's what all mothers say about newborns," she said. "You ask Janey Foster!"

But there was no chance to ask Janey Foster or any of the other grown-ups anything, they were all far too busy doing whatever they do at a birth time—except Granny, and I didn't like asking Granny questions; her answers were always that long they made me wish I had asked someone else.

So I had to talk to Martha.

"Why did she look so cross and wrinkled up, although she was so nice?" I asked.

Martha raised her eyebrows, shrugged her shoulders and grunted. "I didn't see anything nice about her," she said, "but I think they all look crumpled up when they first come. You did."

"Did you see me quite new?" I asked. "Did I look like that one up there?"

"Can't remember," said Martha. "I expect you did."

"Worse, I doubt!" Richard added.

The next night I took myself up to bed real early, and lay there watching the pretty flame of the long candle that burned steadily by the cradle, with my new sister asleep under its hood. I wanted to talk to my mother about her, but she was asleep and they told me I'd be slapped if I woke her up.

Every night after that, every night till our Sarah was christened, Granny rattled on about the lighted candle that was to protect her through the night. And every night I struggled to keep awake to make sure it stayed alight, because sometimes on stormy nights when the wind was blowing straight off the fell, the draft under the roof tiles flickered the flame frighteningly. But every night I fell asleep, and though it was always burning when I woke up in the morning, I sometimes wondered whether Mother, or maybe Father, had wakened in the darkness to find it blown out, and had lit it up again.

After Sarah was safely baptized, and she and Mother were living in the kitchen with the rest of us again, Granny used to stare at Sarah for long minutes on end, just stare and stare and say nothing—no cooing or chattering like people do with babbies—and once I heard her asking Mother if she was quite sure she had never let the candle go out while Sarah was still unbaptized. Mother said of course she was sure, and I don't think my mother ever told lies.

One thing I did wonder long afterward though. I am not sure that Mother or Father would really reckon that Sarah could have been "safely baptized," not with what they would call a proper baptism. Even though what they called the "true religion" was banished, John Duckett had been baptizing children in the Dale secretly into the old faith. But they had caught him on the bank up above our village and sent him to his death at Tyburn for being a priest, three months before Sarah was born. So she, too, had to be christened in the parish church, same as Richard and Martha and me had been. But whether the

Little People understood or took account of the difference between one kind of sprinkling and the other, I cannot tell you.

I only hoped that Sarah would stay with us safely forever. I had always wanted so much to have a little sister.

2

The Little Stone Dollies

O ne of the annoying things that Sarah used to do was to rock herself backward and forward, backward and forward, singing croaky little songs without words (or with words that no mortal could understand) for hours on end. At least, it was annoying to some folk, though it never bothered me overmuch. I couldn't see that it did any harm, and it was better than spilling things, or knocking crockery over, or just getting under everybody's feet, which is what she did most of the rest of the time. No wonder that Mother was always wishing herself in Heaven with the gate shut. She was a real little stop-work, that one! Yet I could not blame Sarah either. She only wanted to do the things she wanted to do, the same as everybody else does. It wasn't her fault she was born clumsy.

But Granny could not abide that rocking. I mind her complaining to our mother about it. I think I was near ten year old at the time, so our Sarah would have been four.

"Why don't she play like other bairns?" Granny grumbled. "You should make her a rag babby, Margaret, leastways she would have something to rock for then, and wouldn't look so daftlike. Folks'll be talking soon enough—them that aren't talking already!"

So Mother made Sarah a rag babby out of an old hood that was threadbare beyond wearing. I think she made it for to keep Granny quiet as much as for giving Sarah a toy to rock. But Sarah would have no truck with it. No sooner had Mother put it in her lap as she sat swaying by the hearthside, than Sarah picked it up by one leg and flung it on the fire.

"Don't want rag babby!" she grunted. "Sarah want little stone dolly for rock-a-bye!"

I was sorry for Mother because she had made a real nice little rag babby out of that hood. I was sorry for the rag babby, and I was sorry for Sarah too when she had her ears boxed for being an ungrateful child.

I knew the afternoon would be uncomfortable for everyone after all that commotion, so it didn't surprise me when Sarah started tugging at my gown and asking me to take her to see the little stone dollies. She always liked to be with them when times were bad at home. Mother expected me to help with the butter making that afternoon and I couldn't get away from it, so I pulled myself free of Sarah and told her to give over.

Of course she followed us into the dairy, where she was under our feet as much or more than she usually was, and being scolded time and again for her clumsiness. So when Mother said, "Lucy, take that child out of here and lose her—back to where she came from, for all I care!" I was glad enough to escape.

We went through that door so fast we all but fell over the redbreast that was hopping around the threshold. We hadn't seen it since the wintertime, when it was forever pecking and twittering at the doorstep.

"Bird!" laughed Sarah as it flew off into the hedge.

Grabbing her by the hand, I ran down the street toward the church. She ran with a funny side-to-side wobble, smiling up at me with her usual clowny smile, and a thread of dribble running down her chin.

I loved Sarah for the way she was nearly always happy and smiling, and the way she always seemed to like me—even when I was in a bad mood, and everyone else hating me. So I never minded the dribble, or the funny noises she made sometimes.

I knew Mother didn't really mean that about losing Sarah. But Mother flared up suddenly when she was vexed, just like Richard and Martha did, and then words came out of them that they had meant to keep inside. Granny said it was their red hair made them that way, and not their fault. All the same, I wished she hadn't said that about where Sarah came from, because it set me wondering whether, after all, even she doubted Sarah was her own human child.

When we reached the churchyard we were both out of breath, and Sarah had the hiccups. Hiccups always made her laugh, so we sat down on the grass to wait for the hiccuping and laughing to be over. It took a long time. There were daisies opening all around, so I began making a chain. I wanted to show Sarah how to do it, but you need fingernails for making daisy chains, and Sarah's nails were bitten down to nothing, and her pudgy fingers got in one another's way. When she found she could not do it, she threw a couple of flowers up in the air in disgust and they landed on her head, so that set her off laughing and hiccuping again.

When at last she was quiet, I slipped my daisy chain over her head and we tiptoed into the church. There, as always, Sir John and Lady Catherine were waiting for us. Up near the chancel they were, made out of stone that I think the priest said was called alabaster, and lying on a sort of table. Him propped up on one elbow as though he were reading in bed—but there wasn't any book—and her at his side with her hands folded, looking very neat and patient.

They were partly so like real people, and partly so different from real, that I was a bit frightened when I looked at them too long—as though maybe he was gazing back at me and might even start breathing, but he never did. The top of Sarah's head only came up to the top of the table, so she was not so troubled as I was by Sir John's staring.

But what Sarah liked, and what I liked, were the seven little children saying their prayers under the table, three little boys facing in one direction and four little girls facing the other way. No wonder Sarah loved those little stone dollies, small as new kittens, and absolutely perfect!

"Hello, dollies! Hello, dollies! Hello, dollies!" she greeted them in a croaky whisper, then, smiling her broad smile, she patted them one by one on the head.

Then, "Lucy tell Sarah dollies' names!" she demanded. Once we had chosen names for all the little stone dollies, but Sarah never could remember them, and I had to repeat them for her every time.

"Robert, Arthur, James, Elizabeth, Hannah, Mary and . . . ?" I always waited for Sarah to fill in the name of the smallest, favorite little girl, the only one she could ever remember.

"Sarah!" she squealed triumphantly. "Sarah! Like me!"

Sarah would have happily spent the rest of the day in church, humming and whispering to the dollies and tickling Lady Catherine's feet, but after a while I thought that Mother would have her temper back again and would be wanting us home.

Sarah made a growling kind of snarl that was the same as swearing in Sarah-language when I said it was time to go back home. She always hated leaving those little stone children. Then, "Good-bye, dollies, Sarah come back soon," she promised, and followed me shuffling toward the porch door. Just as we reached it she turned back.

"Sarah kiss little Sarah-dolly good night. Lucy wait!" she said.

She was not gone long, and when she came running back to me I didn't notice that there was anything different about her.

3

Sarah Is Missing

Next day Martha and I came in for dinner feeling real hungry after weeding among the vegetables all morning. The redbreast that was keeping us company was pecking for grubs and such, finding himself plenty to eat.

Weeding was work I didn't much care for, though it was good to be outside on a day as fine as that was, with the scent of sweet cicely below the hedge, hot sun on the damp earth, the cuckoo shouting away on the other side of the river, and out of earshot of Granny complaining in the kitchen. I did sometimes wish I were a boy, so as I could go to school and get away from all the weeding and farmwork and the scouring of pots and baking and everything else that girls have to do, though Richard never set much store by any of the schooling he had.

I wished it were Sunday, for there was sometimes a bit of meat or bacon for us, Sundays, though often enough it was only meat for Father, even then. The rest of the week it was turnip and salt (or butter sometimes) for everybody, and if the turnips didn't fill us up there would be maslin with butter or honey. Maslin was very firm, hard bread made from a mixture of wheat and rye, and there was no other kind of bread eaten by ordinary folk in Weredale in those days.

"And where's our Sarah at?" Granny snapped at us as soon as we were sat down at the table. I told her I hadn't seen Sarah since breakfast, though I must say I was surprised at myself for not noticing she wasn't with us. She was usually such a clinger.

"Oh!" said Granny in a knowing kind of voice, glaring at Mother. Mother looked worried and startled. I knew fine what Granny was thinking. She was thinking what half our village thought by that time—that our Sarah was a fairy child, a changeling, and if she was not cared for right, the Little People would snatch her back to their fairy home at the first chance, and bring back Mother's own proper human child, as like as not. And I know there were some who thought that Mother should thump Sarah harder than she thumped her already, and more often, and starve her and treat her real badly, so that way the Little People would surely come and rescue her, and we would be rid of Sarah and her dirty habits for good and all.

Yet I never heard Mother say one word of Sarah being a changeling. Nor did I ever hear any of our neighbors suggest such a thing directly in her hearing. But I knew Granny was sure of it. Maybe I never heard her say so outright, but there were plenty of I-told-you-so looks and half-finished sentences that told her meaning.

Mother and Granny were never much afraid of Sarah wandering away and getting lost, because if she were inside, the door was always kept shut and Sarah was too little to reach the sneck; and if she were outside she was sure to be tagging along with me somewhere, and we would both be back home for the next meal. Our stomachs always shouted "pantry" in good time for that.

So now they were trying to find someone to blame for her disappearance, and the likeliest one seemed to be Richard, who could have forgotten to shut the door properly when he set out for school that morning. Of course he denied it. It was just his bad luck that, it being Saturday and a half holiday, he was at home at dinner time and caught the full blast of Granny's temper.

Never mind whose fault it was that she was gone, I was wanting to run and look for Sarah there and then. Whoever she might be, fairy child or human child, I had to find her at once. One thing I was glad about, and that was the daisy chain I had made for Sarah the day before. Funny little Sarah never would take a daisy chain off. She just kept it on indoors, out of doors, in bed, out of bed, till it was that, wilted, it dropped to pieces and fell off her. Moreover, it didn't need Granny or Janey Foster to tell me that wearing a daisy chain was as good a way as any to guard against stealing by the Little People. Of course, I didn't think they would be specially after Sarah, anymore than they'd be after me, or anyone else. All the same, I was glad she was wearing it.

I moved away from the table, but Granny wouldn't have it.

"Time and plenty to seek the bairn after you've eaten them turnips," she said. "She'll not get far in that time if she's not got far already."

I looked at Mother, hoping she would tell me to go, but she was ladling out more turnip for Richard, so I couldn't see her face nor guess what she was thinking. Father was silent, as usual; if you were blind, you'd never have known if he was in the room or not, he was always that quiet.

Richard was telling Martha how he had found a red-breast's nest in the bottom of the hedge with seven eggs in it.

"You leave them eggs alone!" Granny interrupted. "You'll bring trouble to yoursel' if you tak' them!

"The robin and the wren
Are God Almighty's cock and hen;
Him that harries their nest
Never shall his soul have rest."

"Every lad knows that, Granny," said Richard. "You know that lad what used to sit aside me in the school last year? That Jimmy Trotter? He took a nestful of robin's eggs, an' he were dead within the month."

"Aye," she said. "I would expect it."

"But one of them eggs looked different," Richard

went on. "The same size but colored a bit different. Maybe it were dropped by a cuckoo. There'd be no danger takin' that un, likely, but I weren't sure enough to risk it."

"If it were a cuckoo egg you'd leastways be favoring the redbreast by moving it," said Granny. "That egg would hatch out a changeling bird that would hoy the redbreast eggs clear out o' the nest, leavin' room only for its big ugly greedy sel'. We don't want no changelings here! Inside the house, nor out, birds nor bairns!"

She looked hard at Mother, who didn't look up. Martha didn't seem to be listening; she wasn't interested in anything except getting food inside herself as fast as she could.

I couldn't wait any longer. I couldn't bear to hear any more of that changeling talk. I just had to find Sarah.

"I'll take some maslin and eat as I go," I said, and I put two big hunks of it in my pocket, one for Sarah, one for me.

As I ran out the door, Granny was still complaining that I was leaving the table before we had said grace, but Mother said nothing, so likely she wanted me to go. For the sake of peace she never contradicted Granny if her own temper could hold out, but I generally knew when she didn't agree.

It was easy for me to guess where Sarah might have gone. I ran straight there. The door of the church was closed. Sarah could not have opened or closed that heavy door by herself, but I had to go inside and look, even so. I felt so sure that that was where she would be.

When the great door had finished creaking, there was a dead silence in the church, but for my own breathing. And not a sight of Sarah.

It must have been the first time that I had been in the church all by myself—except that I didn't feel by myself with Sir John looking as though the creaking door had disturbed his thoughts and he was just about to ask me what my business was. It seemed much bigger and colder and dimmer in there than it had ever been before.

I made up my mind to walk right around Sir John and Lady Catherine, and look behind every pillar before I came out. But I really knew already that she wasn't there. You could never be in any place with our Sarah without you could hear her breathing. A terrible noisy breather she was, with that snuffy nose of hers, and her bad chest. Richard used to grumble that sleeping in the loft with her was no better than being in a pigsty with a litter of snoring pigs, she made that much noise.

So I took a deep breath and looked Sir John right in the eye in a bolder way than I had ever looked at him before. Then I walked straight down to where he was.

It was all just as it had been before. Sir John looking strict and haughty on top there, with Lady Catherine asleep, or pretending to be asleep, and the seven little children underneath saying their prayers, or pretending to say their prayers. But no! This time they were not quite all as they had been before. The smallest girl, the one we called Sarah, was wearing a withering daisy chain on top of the old-fashioned ruff that stuck out from her neck like a great dinner platter. Of course the chain was much too big for the little stone girl, and it reached down far below where her knees would have been if you could have seen her knees beneath her alabaster gown, yet she looked happy to be wearing it. I had a feeling that if Sir John could have seen her, he would have told her to take it off and not be such a silly little girl. So I was glad she was safely out of his sight under the table there.

I walked right around to the other side of them. Sarah was not there, but I pulled the ugliest face I could make at the back of Sir John's head while I was about it, and that made me feel a little better.

Then I looked in every dark hiding-hole that I could think of—up in the pulpit, behind some old vestments in the vestry that had not been locked away, and under-neath all the seats in the choir stalls. I found all sorts of funny things there that I didn't know about before— flowers and fruit and animals and birds as well as people. I would have liked to show them all to Sarah. I was glad the Parliament soldiers had not spoiled any of it that time they came to Wulsingham and arrested John Duckett.

But now the war was beginning again, and our Rich-ard always hoping that when the militia was called out he would be thought tall enough to go fighting for Crom-well. So he was forever seeking in the copse for sticks long enough to use as a pike, and playing at soldiering with himself or his friends at every odd moment when they weren't bird's-nesting.

Well, I went on searching and searching because I felt so sure that Sarah must have been in the church that morning to put her chain on the stone dolly. Though how she got in and out through that heavy porch door is something I could not understand.

I was just wondering if I dared go up the twisty little staircase to the bell tower where the bats lived, when I remembered her going back to say good night to the little stone Sarah on the day before. So, likely, that would be when she put the necklace on the dolly. That would do away with the puzzle of how she got into the church that morning. But it would do away, too, with the protection of the daisies for herself, if she had really been out ever since Richard had set off for school that morning. I felt very frightened for her.

4

Sarah Is Not Telling

I ran straight out of the church, past the grammar school, where I could hear the boys gabbling their lessons inside, and on down to the river. We played there sometimes, splashing stones into the water, and just now the bright yellow monkey musk flowers that Sarah was so fond of picking were full out among the stones at the water's edge. So I thought that was where she'd be.

The river was running deep and fast after the heavy rain we had been having. It could be treacherous down there, and Sarah had no sense, no sense at all. She toppled over so easily, too, walking over those big round stones in her clogs.

Old George Charlton was fishing by the bridge where we usually played. I asked him if he had seen Sarah, but he didn't hear me, so I shouted, and then shouted again louder, till at last he said, "Sarah? Who is Sarah?"

"My sister," I shouted, "my little sister Sarah. Have you seen her?"

"Oh, the little half-wit!" he said, shaking his head.

"You call her Sarah, do you? She'll need some looking after, that one! She's not bin here. I bin here all day. No one's bin down here frightening the fishes till you come!"

I thanked him and apologized for frightening his fishes, though it wasn't my fault he was so deaf that I had to shout, was it? There was certainly no sign of Sarah having been there. The musk flowers were quite untouched; when Sarah picked anything she always dropped near as much as she carried away.

I ran along the riverside path for a while, still seeing no sign of Sarah, though if she had fallen into the water she could have been carried away for miles, leaving no mark behind, the flood was hurrying that fast—brown, peaty water from the moors swirling the feathery ropes of foam like Peg Powler's suds. Right on to Bishops Aukland it was running, then to the city of Durham, and, after that, to the sea. That's what people said.

But I had never been to any of those places. I could not say how far away they were, or how long it would take me to get there. I only knew that the river was moving much faster than I was, and would reach anyplace first, and if the river had caught Sarah, it would be too late when I found her.

I was out of breath when I saw old Minnie Ward coming along the river path. Minnie used to be a Wise Woman years ago, my mother said. Well, I suppose she was still a Wise Woman, because once you had the knowledge you would have it for always, wouldn't you? But folk reckoned she didn't know near as much as Janey

Foster knew, and Janey always cheerful and civil with it too. So when anyone had any kind of trouble, it was natural that Janey would be the one they would run to for help. The knocking on Minnie Ward's door grew less and less over the years.

Minnie seldom stirred out of her cottage, and I had never met her when I was all by myself before. I was not frightened, because I was sure she wasn't a witch, even though a few old gossips said that was what she could be. But I wished, all the same, that I had met her in the village where there would be people and houses round about, instead of just the two of us quiet down there on the river path. I stepped aside to let her pass with her stiff legs and her stick and her wide petticoats. She stood still and stared at me.

"You are out of breath, young woman," she said. "What are you hurrying for?"

"Sarah," I said. "My sister Sarah has disappeared. Have you seen her anywhere?" As soon as I had asked, I wished I hadn't.

The old woman shrugged her shoulders, gazing straight ahead.

"So They have come for her at last?" she said. "I looked for Them taking her back long before this."

I knew fine what she meant, but I didn't believe what she believed, nor think what she thought. But I was not going to have an argue with her, so I just wished her good day and hurried on.

I could have gone on running along by the river for-

ever without finding Sarah, and I was fair racked with
wondering what to do, or where to seek for the best,
when I saw Charity Maddison running down the path
that led back into the east end of the village. Charity was
older than I was, but she hadn't started working for anyone yet.

She waved as soon as she saw me, and I ran to meet
her. We both spoke together. I said, "Have you seen our
Sarah?" and she said, "Where've you bin?"

Charity laughed and said, "Why, aye! I was talking to
her just a few minutes gone, back in the churchyard. I
thought you would be with her, or nearby, but when I
couldn't see you I asked her where you were. She
wouldn't say anything, leastways nowt that I could make
any sense on. She do talk funny, that bairn, don't she?"

"Did you leave her there all by herself?" I asked.

Charity nodded. "I'd have taken her back to your
mother, but she wouldn't come with me, so I were looking for you or Martha." That's what she said. But what
she meant was she durstn't go to our cottage because of
our Granny's scolding tongue. She was a real timid one,
that Charity, in some ways; other ways she was bold as a
ferret.

We ran back into the village. Charity turned right,
knowing fine well that she was already late for the milking and her father would be vexed. I turned left toward
the marketplace, straight past our cottage without looking at it, and then on up to the church. I did not stop to
speak to anyone on the way, just hurried past them.

I could not see Sarah in the churchyard as I went through the gate. The porch door was closed, just as I had left it. I ran to the back of the church, the north side, and there, sitting in the long grass, pulling a buttercup to pieces, was Sarah.

She looked up and saw me, and smiled happily.

"Lucy come back," she said as though we had parted only a minute or two ago, and turned her attention to her buttercup again.

"Lucy didn't run away!" I said. "It's Sarah what has run away! Where've you been, Sarah?"

Sarah looked at me with her mouth open. I would never have anyone else say so, but that bairn did look uncommonly stupid sometimes.

Her answer came slowly, and it made me feel cold and shaky when she said, "Bin playing with little people."

Well, that's what it sounded like, but she never did speak clearly, our Sarah, so I tried to hope she had said something different.

"What did you say, Sarah?" I asked.

"Bin playin' with little people," she repeated as clearly as she ever said anything.

"What little people?" I asked. "Where are they? How did you find them? Have you seen them before? Did you take anything to eat from them?" I asked all in one breath, which was foolish of me, because Sarah could only ever understand one question at a time, if she understood that, but I was so frightened for her that I wanted to know everything at once.

Sarah smiled widely again. "Not telling" was all she said.

I had to know that it wasn't the fairies that Sarah had been playing with. But I durstn't ask her straight out because in those days when we were children, and when everyone believed in the Little People, we knew how they hated to be named, and would mischief them that did so. That is why we always used to call them "Them" or "Little People" or "Little Folk." These days are different, with the preachers telling us that the Nameless Ones are just pagan superstition, and some clever ones saying there are no such beings, nor never were. Come to think on it, 'tis a wonder I ever knew the word "fairy" when I was a bairn, folk were that careful not to speak it. Yet I did know it, and I reckon it was like all the other bad words we were told we shouldn't ever say. Some bold or careless body was sure to say them, and those words were the words we were surest to hear, and remember.

Maybe, though, it wasn't Them that Sarah had been playing with. Children were little people, weren't they? There were Widow Nattress's bairns—three or four of them were really small and always toddling around loose for Sarah or anyone else to play with if they wanted to. And there were plenty of others in Wulsingham you might well call little people; there were the stone dollies under Sir John's table in the church. They were surely little people, if any were. Perhaps she had been back to the church by herself, after all. If she had, it was doubtless the little dollies she would be meaning.

Besides, if Sarah were one of their own, as some said she was, the fairies would have taken her back forever, wouldn't they? And if she were human, they'd have stolen her for seven years at least, just for spying on them. When they stole humans it was always for seven years at a time. Seven and seven times seven it could be.

"Were you playing with little people here, in the churchyard?" I asked, knowing well that They usually kept distant from holy places. But I was saying anything I could think of to make her talk and tell me more.

"Not telling!" Sarah laughed, and I knew then that I would not get the truth out of her that day, if ever I got it out at all. The more I went on asking, the more she would go on not telling, and enjoying the joke of it.

It was not often I felt angry with Sarah, but I felt angry then, and I wanted to shake her, and shake her hard.

But there would be plenty of scolding, or worse, when we got home. Half of me was wanting to hurry home at once where I knew Mother would be waiting anxiously for news of Sarah. The other half of me wanted to stay away forever from Granny's questions and opinions, and Richard's silly remarks. In any case, I wanted time to think what to say when all the questioning began, so I gave Sarah my hands and pulled her up.

"Come on, Sarah!" I said. "I'll show you something nice I've found in here before we go home. But first I'll make you a beautiful new necklace."

We ran around to the sunny side of the church, where

the daisies were growing red-tipped and in plenty, and I made a fine long chain for her.

That cuckoo across the river was still calling. It had been at it all day. Sarah seemed to hear it for the first time.

"Cuck-oo! Cuck-oo!" she laughed. "Funny bird!"

"It's a silly, nasty bird!" I said.

Sarah laughed again. "*Funny* bird, funny, like Sarah! Cuck-oo, cuck-oo!"

"There you are!" I said, holding the daisy chain out to her. "Put that on, and keep it on till tomorrow, when I'll make you another. I'll make one for you every day, no matter how busy I am."

She put it on, and, holding hands tightly, we went into the church together.

5

The Pig in Church

So now, there we were, back in the church, with Sarah tugging me toward the family of little stone children. Anything I wanted to show her would have to wait till she had seen them again.

"Hello, dollies!" she said, patting them all as usual.

I had left the withered daisy chain where it was, around the smallest girl's neck, and Sarah pulled at it so that it fell to the floor.

"Dead now!" she said. "Little dolly have new one," and she tried clumsily to take off the chain I had just made for her.

"No, Sarah! That one is for you!" I said, trying to stop her, but she tugged at it so roughly that it broke and swung loosely around her neck life a scarf.

"Look!" I explained. "Lucy will make two chains, one for Sarah-dolly and one for Sarah Emerson."

The chain had been long enough to make one for each of them out of it. Sarah watched, grunting impatiently while I divided it, but was happy enough when I had finished.

"Now Lucy tell Sarah dollies' names!" She smiled hopefully.

As fast as I could I named Robert, Arthur, James, Elizabeth . . .

"Lucy make chain for Elizabeth!" interrupted Sarah.

"No, Sarah!" I answered firmly, for without doubt she would be insisting on finding more daisies, and not satisfied till Hannah and Mary were jeweled with flowers, and the boys as well, likely, so we would never get home.

"Come, Sarah, see who's hiding under the seats here," I said, pulling her muttering into the choir.

The sun was shining through the chancel windows, so it was much lighter in the choir stalls than it had been there earlier in the day when I was looking for Sarah underneath the seats, and I could see much more clearly all the lively busyness that was going on down there.

I knew Sarah would enjoy all those wooden hares and other curious little creatures—those two, for instance, that looked as though they were running into one another, and into bad trouble as well; the guilty-looking fox with the goose between its jaws, and the great bristling porker escaping from the hunter, right next to it. Beyond the swine a fancily dressed young man was playing the tabor for all he was worth; and after him a man was pushing his wife in a wheelbarrow not nearly big enough for her. Then a happy monk with a fish, and great bunches of grapes, grapes as big as crab apples, and some extravagant birds. I tried for a long time to decide whether one of them was a goose or a peahen.

Then, right down at the far end, nearest to the altar, was my sister Sarah on all fours trying to stare out a shaggy bear; and the bear, chained and standing on its hind legs, was trying to stare out Sarah. I suppose I ought not to have let go of her hand, but I thought she would be happy enough to keep out of mischief looking at all those creatures down there. So I sat down on the altar steps for a few peaceful minutes to think out what I was going to say at home, and how to stop Sarah babbling on about Little People when they started on the questions. I wanted her to babble to me, but not to them.

It was quiet and peaceful down there only till Sarah started barking.

I moved over to her and said "Shhhhhhhhhhhh!" but she went on barking. I put my hand on her shoulder and tried to pull her up. She sat back on her heels and pointed to the bear.

"Big dog," she said.

"No," I told her. "It's not a big dog. It's a big bear. And you mustn't be a dog in church."

"Dog-in-church!" she said. "Bad dog-in-church, bad bear, go outside!" Then she noticed some sort of a bird carved in the foliage above the bear.

After that she dropped on all fours again, and went shuffling down along the row till she came to the swine seat.

"Pig-in-church! Bad pig-in-church!" she scolded. She started grunting and slavering so that I knew I had made a stupid mistake in showing her those comical seat carvings just then. It would likely be hard work getting her out of the choir stalls and back home. Obstinate as a mule our Sarah was when she wanted to be.

Somehow I managed to pull and push her out of the chancel and into the nave. If we turned left we might be able to go down the south aisle, sneaking past Sir John and Lady Catherine without her seeing the little stone dollies on the other side, but not very likely; far better to turn right down the north aisle and miss them altogether, even though it was a longer way around. We would be out much quicker if she didn't see them. So, keeping tight hold of her hand, I turned down to the right.

But I couldn't fool Sarah. She was not always as stupid as she made out she was, that one.

"Wrong way!" She laughed good-naturedly, pulling me back. "Silly Lucy! Little dollies this way!"

So back we had to go, and name the little dollies all over again, and say good-bye to each in turn, and re-arrange Sarah-dolly's daisy chain before we were able to leave the church, or else there would have been pandemonium such as never was!

I had to pull Sarah along the road to our cottage as she rocked rhythmically from side to side, singing huskily:

> "Pig-in-church, pig-in-church,
> Bad, bad,
> Pig-in-church!"

I thought she would surely be wanting to get home for something to eat, if for nothing else. She always had a big appetite, did our Sarah, and it was not like her to miss her dinner without complaining.

"Aren't you hungry, Sarah?" I asked, hoping to hurry her forward a little, but she just shook her head and stroked her stomach.

"Not hungry now," she said.

"Did the Little People give you something to eat?" I asked, but before the words were all out of my mouth I guessed she would not be telling, and I guessed right.

Granny, by Heaven's grace, was sound asleep in her chair when we got home. Mother was in one of her irritable moods, but not so bad that she couldn't see the sense in keeping Granny asleep. So we were no sooner well inside our door than she pushed us out again without a word spoken. With her finger on her lips and a nod toward Granny she followed us out into the yard.

"And so where did you find her?" she asked, cuffing Sarah around the ear so as to let out some of the anger and worry that had been boiling up inside her all afternoon.

"She was only in the churchyard," I answered. "She had been picking buttercups all by herself in there."

"There are plenty of buttercups at our own door," snapped Mother, "without you going down to the church to pick 'em! You bin in the churchyard all day long? Where else you bin?"

Sarah stared blankly in front of her, not only not tell-ing, but not even speaking.

I kept quiet about going to the church earlier in the afternoon and not finding her there. After all, she could well have been behind the church with her buttercups then, and me not seeing her, I've no doubt. So I just said that Sarah had kept on not telling, the way she often did, but Charity Maddison had seen her in the churchyard before I did, so likely she had been there all the time.

That set Mother on to saying what she thought about Charity for not fetching the bairn home, and I let her prattle on about it till some of the anger had gone out of her, and she finished with asking Sarah if she weren't hungry after this long time. She went indoors to fetch a bite for her, telling me to keep a good eye on her till she came back.

Sarah sat down in the yard, leaning her back against the house wall, and began sucking her fingers the way she always did before she went to sleep. When Mother came back with some oatcake for her, Sarah's eyes were all but shut. She must have been fair tired out. I wished I knew where she had been, and what she had been doing.

Of course Mother was vexed when Sarah didn't eat the oatcake after she had been tiptoeing so carefully around the kitchen to get it without waking Granny. Sometimes I used to wonder if I would be so scared of dis-turbing Mother's temper when I was a grown woman as Mother was of unsettling Granny when we were young.

Then Mother calmed right down and said, "That poor, weary bairn might as well be in bed and out of the road when all the others come in, leastways we'll know where she is then. 'Young uns sleep theirsel's better,' you know." It was just the sort of thing that Granny used to say. Then she added, "We'll get her up the ladder now, between us."

I was glad to hear her talking that way about Sarah. I knew she was really fond of her underneath. It was just the sharp tongue she had, and the way she thought other people were forever nudging and whispering about where Sarah came from that made her waspish.

So between us we managed to push Sarah up the ladder and lay her on our pallet, where she was soon snoring loud enough to rouse old Granny, down there in the kitchen beneath, ten times over.

Strangely enough, Granny stayed asleep all through that evening.

6

Sarah Is Left Behind

*G*ranny never did wake up.

We were all shocked next morning when we found her cold and stiff in her chair. She must have slept herself away down there in the kitchen, in the way she had always told us that "young uns sleep theirsel's better, and old uns sleep theirsel's away." She was seventy-one year old when she slept hersel' away so peacefully there at the fireside, and that was a great age to be.

For a few days we forgot about her complaining, and only remembered the times between, and the things she used to make for us, and how good her baking always tasted. It was strange the way I had so often longed for her not to live with us anymore, but when she was gone, away down there in the graveyard, I felt lonely for her and wished she could be back by our hearthside.

One result of Granny sleeping away just when she did was that there was so much talk of Granny and her burying that there were not so many questions asked about Sarah and where she had been. Mother and I were seemingly the only ones who noticed her at all during that

week, Mother flaring up with, "Where's our Sarah at?"
or "What's that bairn doing now?" at the most solemn
and unsuitable moments; and me never leaving Sarah's
side until after the funeral was over, and making sure she
was never without a daisy chain, and wondering what I
should do when their flowering time was over. I remember finding three daisies once, on Christmas Eve, and
Charity had said that there were always one or two somewhere right through the year if you kept looking. But not
enough to make a chain, that I did know.

One day a week or two later I remembered the nest
that Richard had been talking about on the day that
Sarah was lost. The shock and fluster of that week had
sent it out of my mind. Thinking to give Mother five
minutes' peace, I told her I would take Sarah down to the
garden hedge to see if we could find it. Sarah, of course,
was very eager to go with me.

The only nest that I could find, near the bottom of the
hedge there, was full of a great ugly naked pale wriggling
thing, bigger than a full-grown redbreast, I should say.
Richard had shown me a nest of young redbreasts the
year before, and they were ugly enough, and no more like
to grown redbreasts than I am. But this creature was bigger, and worse than them. It must have been a cuckoo,
like Granny had said. There were broken eggshells on
the ground below and not a sign of any other nestlings,
so likely that horrid bird had pushed them out of the nest
before they had a chance to hatch.

"I think it's a cuckoo," I said to Sarah.

"Cuck-oo, cuck-oo," she repeated hopefully a dozen times. Then, finding the dumb creature did not reply, she laughed and said, "Cuckoo not talking! Sarah can say 'Cuck-oo!' That one not a real cuckoo. Sarah is a cuckoo!"

"Sarah is *not* a cuckoo," I answered sharply. "Sarah is a little girl, a little *human* girl."

"Sarah is a cuckoo," she insisted. "Cuck-oo! Cuck-oo!"

Away across the river, a bird called, "Cuck-oo! Cuck-oo!"

"Cuck-oo!" Sarah answered it.

I wished Granny had never said that about the cuckoo being a changeling bird. I could never get it out of my head.

Months later the daisies dwindled and disappeared. It didn't really matter, though, for all through that winter, until the lambing started and the celandines were out again, Sarah stayed safely indoors, weekdays, rocking and singing at the fireside. I tried to teach her to knit once, but she was forever pulling it back and dropping loops, so that Mother said she had neither wool nor time to spin it just for making tangles like that.

If Sarah remembered anything about the "Little People," she spoke no more of them. She even seemed to have lost a little of her interest in the stone dollies as well, though we saw them when we were taken to church every Sunday through the cruelest weather.

At last the days grew warmer and longer again, and we were much more outside, picking daisies and seeing all the new things that were coming. Father was a shepherd, so he was busy with lambing on the fellside, and nearer home there were ducklings and chickens for Sarah and me to see after.

When that long spring gave way to high summer, our Martha went in place to a big farm above Frosterley. She was glad enough to be grown up and away from home, I think, though I guess there was plenty of hard work for her there. Martha didn't mind hard work though, not like Charity Maddison.

I think our mother missed Martha badly that summer, although she never said much about her being away except that at least there was one less mouth to feed. So it did not surprise me that, come September, she told me she could manage without my help for one day, and I could walk over to the farm where Martha was, and take her a few things she might be needing, and I could find out if she was looking well and being rightly fed and not worked beyond her strength.

"Our Sarah can stay with me," she said. "It is a full four mile there, and the four mile back will feel like ten. That is over-far for such a bairn."

"Sarah go with Lucy!" said Sarah happily. She was sitting in a corner of the kitchen playing with the rolling pin. It happened so often that when you thought she wasn't hearing she understood more than when you spoke directly to her, loud and plainly.

So there were Mother and Sarah having a fratch, with me in the middle of it not knowing which course I favored for the best. I knew it was a long way for Sarah to go, long enough for me, let alone her. But I knew the trouble she would be in the kitchen with Mother baking the bread that morning, and being far on with another baby coming. I knew that, tired or not, I would have enjoyed having Sarah for company most of the day, which is more than Mother would.

But it was by myself I went in the end, knowing fine well that Sarah would be in a stubborn mood, and Mother with little enough patience to spare for her, and the road to Martha's farm stretching lonely in front of me.

So I was glad enough to see Charity dawdling along ahead of me soon after I left home. She was taking some cheese to her grandmother who lived on the Frosterley road, she said, and there'd be plenty harder work waiting for her when she got home, so no wonder she was taking her time.

"And what you got there? An' where you taking it?" she asked, pointing to the wool skeins I had hapt up in an apron, under my arm.

"Wool," I said, "and a few sweetmeats for Martha. She's in place in a farm up above Frosterley. John Turnbull they call the farmer."

"Oh aye!" said Charity. "Him! I've heard my grand-mother speak of him. A Roundhead, that's what he is! As strait a Puritan as there ever was!" and she spat on the ground to show what she thought about Roundheads.

Charity had been spitting about Roundheads ever since King Charles had been executed early in the previous year, for all that her own mother and father were themselves zealous Puritans. Most of the farmers and other people round about us were Royalists. I think my parents were Royalists, but I wasn't really sure at that age because they never talked about it, and my father, especially, was that quiet he rarely spoke a word about anything, for or against. Neither did they discourage Richard when he kept on talking about how he was going to join Cromwell's army the minute he was tall enough and old enough.

Myself, I didn't understand enough to get angry on either side, not like Charity or Richard did, anyway. I couldn't untangle all the argument about popish priests and Independents and Covenanters neither, for there seemed to be good and evil ones scrambled in among all of them for all that I could see. But the war was a bad time every way for all opinions, with the men being taken away by the militia and the women hard put to it to keep the farms going on their own, and find food for soldiers, never mind their own families. There was damage and trouble caused by soldiers, both sides, burning and destroying everything that lay in the path of battle, and spoiling churches and everything. I prayed Heaven there would be no battle close to Wulsingham.

Then Charity started singing. She had a good, clear voice and we sang together all the songs we could think of, passing the time quickly and cheerfully enough till we came to her grandmother's cottage. There I left her to make the rest of my way alone to the Turnbull farm.

7

Holes

The warm September sun was well up over the fells when I left Charity. We had been singing together so merrily that it wasn't till I was alone that I heard the droning of the bees in the dry grasses and was aware of the ewes bleating from the high moors. The long, dark brown seeds of sweet cicely flowers, still on their tall stems, lined the road edge. I broke off a handful of them, rubbing them between my palms so that my hands smelled of aniseed cakes, reminding me that I was beginning to feel hungry.

It was not long before I was in Frosterley. I had been there once before when I was just a little bairn. Father had had something or other to see to in Frosterley, and he had taken me in front of him on Uncle William's horse that he had borrowed for the day. I remembered how fine the village had looked from that height, with me sitting up there like a real lady.

This time there were not many people to be seen in the long street, and I suppose that I did not know the name or anything at all about any of the few people that I did see moving about.

Two or three small children were playing on the green in front of an open door. They stopped their game to stare as I passed, and a boy put his tongue out at me.

At the far end of the green an old woman came out of a cottage to feed six hens that were scratching around the threshold. Before I left home I had been given directions for finding the Turnbull farm, and I had not forgotten them. But I felt lonely enough to want to talk to anybody about anything. The old gammer had a kind face, so I went up to her and asked the way to the Turnbulls.

She took me around the back of her cottage and pointed out the farm, some long way up the fellside, with a path leading straight to it.

"Keep on yon trod all the way," she said, "and it will take you straight to Turnbulls. Don't go wandering right- or left-ways, mind! There's holes in them rocks!"

Low down, on the right of the path, I thought I could see where the limestone broke out in a little gully. I supposed those were the rocks she meant.

"Holes?" I asked.

"Aye! Holes! Holes you could twist your foot in should you slip, holes you could drop summat in and lose it forever. You should always keep away from holes in rocks."

I wondered why she had warned so sternly about holes in the rocks, and I remembered Martha telling me once that updale at Stanhope there were caves in the limestone where Little People lived, and how some who had spied on them there had come to a bad end.

She asked if I was a relation of John Turnbull, for she knew the Turnbulls well but had never heard of a cousin or a niece or any such of my age in the dale.

So I told her about Martha, and she said, "Oh aye! I heard they had a new girl there called Martha Emerson. They say she is a good lass. Would you like a sup of goat's milk before you go climbing up yonder?"

She went inside and came back with a little cup of milk; fresh, warm and sweet it was, and me very thirsty, so I wished I were bold enough to ask if I might have another one when that was drunk. But I wasn't, so I just thanked her, wished her a very good morning and set off up the hill.

The steepness of the trod slowed me down. Presently I was aware of a singing somewhere away down on the right. Very light it was, and quiet, but clear, though not with any words to it, or not any such as I have heard before or could understand. I stopped a minute for breath and better hearing of it. It seemed to be coming from that gully I had seen from the back of the cottage. Perhaps it was just the burn talking to itself as it tumbled down over the stones, or perhaps it was voices carried far on the wind, children singing at their games away down there in the village, or some bird far out of sight — though likely not that. Yet, louder than the music I could hear the old woman's warning in my head. "Holes! You should always keep away from holes in rocks!"

Though my head was telling me to keep away from

holes, my feet were telling me to run toward them just to keek at them, not close enough to twist my foot in or drop summat down them, and then run back to the trod with no harm done.

I turned around and looked back the way I had come. It was as I expected. The old woman was standing in her garden staring up at me, watching to see I didn't stray away from the trod, I expect. I waved to her. She waved back. I turned again and went on trudging. The singing quieted as I went higher. If I went farther I would lose it altogether. I looked back again. The old woman had disappeared. If she had gone into her cottage she could still be watching through that little window. I didn't care, though. She couldn't stop me leaving the path just a little way if I wanted to.

As fast as a hare I ran to the gully and looked down into it. It was deeper than I thought it would be, and lined with rocks, all jostling higgledy-piggledy out of the ground, with the burn gabbling splashily along the bottom of it. I could hear no other sound but that of my own breathlessness. I put my ear down to the ground and thought I could hear fiddling and singing, the way they say you can when you listen on fairy hills. But no one had ever said anything about fairy hills at Frosterley. I listened again for that music, and thought that perhaps I had only imagined it after all.

It was a very pretty place, with silvery lichens on the rocks like round moons, and small ferns poking out of cracks, and the pinkness of some late thyme.

The gammer had been right about those holes. There was one right opposite me, tall and narrow like the entrance to a cave going straight into the hillside. It was too narrow for anyone to go in, though, even someone as small as Sarah. There was another, even smaller hole that seemed to go straight down into the earth forever. I supposed that was the sort you could drop something down and never find it again.

I wanted to go down the gully and across the burn to look into that cave hole on the other side. My feet wanted to go, anyway, but I kept thinking about those that spied on the Little People in the Linkirk caves at Stanhope, and I fell to wondering what bad end they had come to, for Martha had not told me that part of the story. I thought, too, of that kind old woman down there whose gentle face had become so severe when she told me to keep away from holes. So my fear and my curiosity were having a tug-o'-war inside me, and it was my fear that won in the end, else I might not have been here to tell all this today.

I turned my back on the holes, and set off running back to the trod, listening all the time, but hearing nothing but the humming of insects and an occasional bleating, till I reached the Turnbull farm.

A young woman was filling a trough with a bucket. I asked her for Martha Emerson. She looked at me and laughed.

"I know who *you* are," she said. "You're Martha's little sister Lucy, aren't you?"

I nodded.

"Martha's telled me plenty about you," she said. "And where's your Sarah at? Martha says she follows you around like your own shadow."

I said, "She's been left behind with our mother. It was ower-far for her to come here."

"Oh!" she said. "I thought perhaps They had . . ." But she never finished saying what she thought. People often didn't finish what they'd started saying about Sarah.

"I'll tell Martha you're here," she said instead.

When Prue Turnbull (for that's who the young woman was) came out of the house with our Martha, I was that glad to see Martha that I quite surprised myself. Of course there had been double work for me at home after she had gone, though there were plenty of other things we were always fratching on about when she was home, let alone the bed-kicking. Martha seemed pleased enough to see me, too, and that was a change. When she had asked after everyone else, Mother and Father and Richard, and the goat and the sheep and the chickens and the ducklings, she even asked if our Sarah was well.

I gave Martha the wool, which pleased her, for she loved to be knitting, and before I had done with all the gossip, Prue said she must be getting on with her work now. So Martha blushed, which was uncommon in Martha, and said she must be getting on, too, with whatever she had been doing up at the house.

I had brought some cheese and maslin with me which I

had minded to eat on the way home, but feeling so hungry and seeing it so pleasant and sunny just outside the yard there, I thought I'd sit in the field to eat it before I left. I was sorry to have to say good-bye to Martha so soon, as I watched the two of them running back to the farmhouse.

I had no sooner sat down than back came Martha to tell me that old Mistress Turnbull had said never mind the cheese and bread, I could have a proper hot dinner with all of them when the time came; and until then Martha could have holiday with me, seeing she had worked so hard and willingly these past few weeks and not seen anyone from home in all that time. I was glad then to have Martha sit down beside me, and a chance to hear what she had to tell about the Turnbulls and the farm and everything. It seemed like she was well pleased with the place and being kindly treated.

When she had finished telling, I asked her if she knew anything of the old woman who lived below the farm, down there at the far end of Frosterley, the one who had given me the goat's milk and warned me of holes in the rocks.

Martha shook her head. "I've never spoken with her, though I know who you're meaning. She would be thinking of Little People living in caves like them at Clints Crags and Linkirk. But I've heard nowt about any such in caves hearabouts. Yon old body must be one of them that'll believe any story she can hear, and make up what she can't hear, likely."

I told her then about the music I had heard on the fell-side that morning, how it came and went, and how clearly I heard it when I put my ear to the ground down there in the gully.

Martha smiled the way she often smiled when she thought I was too young to know any better.

"All you could hear," she said, "with your ear to the grass would be grasshoppers and bumler bees. Grasshoppers and bumlers fiddling and piping and singing!"

"But Martha," I said, "those caves you told me about up Stanhope way, what happened to them that spied on the Little People there?"

Martha looked uneasy for a moment.

"Nowt," she said. "Just gossip and milkmaids' tales. There's people always imagining more about Little People than what there really is. Turnbulls don't even believe there are such folk, nor never were."

That seemed very odd to me. They were the first I had ever heard of who didn't believe in the Little Folk. I didn't believe everything I heard about them myself, but I didn't see how anyone could doubt there were such creatures.

The Turnbull family made me very welcome, and it was a real good meal they gave me, though the grace John Turnbull said for it was the most tedious I had ever heard, and there was another one as long to match it at the end.

When it was done I said good-bye to Martha again and was just setting off down the hillside when old Mistress Turnbull came bustling out with a kerchief of plums for me to take home. She told Martha she could set me on my way home a distance, so as her company would shorten the journey for me a little. It certainly did, and with Martha beside me till I was well on the Wulsingham road there was no temptation to turn aside again to explore the mysterious holes. I listened carefully as we came down the trod but could hear no singing, though maybe Martha's chattering would drown any other sound. Neither did I see any sign of the old woman as we passed her cottage.

8

Breeches Don't Blow Out!

I was surprised to find the door standing open when I reached home, and the first person I saw there was Janey Foster, building up the fire in our kitchen.

"So there you are at last!" she said. "Here am I waiting to get away home, and thinking you were never coming!"

"Why?" I asked stupidly. "But what are you doing here?"

Janey laughed. "What does Janey Foster do in other folks' houses, but see to them that's being born, or sick, or dying? And there's no one dying in this house," she added quickly, thinking maybe I'd be feeling anxious.

"But," I said, "the babby? It won't be coming yet? Nor for a month or more, I thought . . ."

Janey laughed again. "Thinking and reckoning's one thing. Coming's quite another. It allus were that way with babbies, and I reckon it allus will be. That Sarah o' yours hurried her along before her time . . . under your mother's feet she was, as usual, the stupid . . . Sent your poor mother sprawling over the floor! By God's good grace they were in the loft at the time, else we'd have never got her safe up to bed."

"But how did you know?" I asked. "Who fetched you? Surely Sarah didn't . . ."

"No, Sarah didn't come running for me," Janey answered sarcastically. "But by good fortune Betsy Greenwell came to borrow summat from your mother—salt I think she said it was. You know how Betsy's allus short on whatever other folks take good care to keep by them, and knowing fine well how unlucky it is to return salt, she'd be certain your mother'd never ax for it back. And with the door being bolted she started rattling the sneck, with nothing happening till your Sarah started shouting and hammering on the other side . . . and that Betsy not able to understand one word of what she were trying to say, till it came to her that maybe there were something badly amiss inside. So she fetches her Tom, an' he brings his tools along an' forces the door for her. Then, when they saw the way things were, Tom came running for me fast enough, and just in time! Your mother's sleeping peacefully now, and mind you let her stay asleep! So you go softly up that ladder, Lucy Emerson, and have one wee keek at your other little sister. She's a proper bairn this time, and no mistake! Small, but good. I've set the candle burning up there, and I found a pair of your father's auld breeches to put beside the bairn, so I'll be away home now."

"But what does a little girl bairn want with a big man's breeches?" I asked.

"Same as a candle," said Janey. "If it had been a lad, we'd have put a petticoat beside him."

"But there were no breeches for Sarah," I objected.

"Your father had but one pair that time, if I mind rightly, and he needed them. He must have had a new pair since then, these auld uns were hanging on a rail in the rafters. Sarah only had a candle, but I'm making double sure this time. Breeches don't blow out!"

Yet it seemed strange, all the same, that I had never heard Granny speak of breeches, for she always seemed to know as much about precautions and charms and such things as Wise Women themselves.

"But Sarah," I said, "where is Sarah?"

Janey looked vaguely around the kitchen. She was quite unworried.

"Up to some mischief, someplace, I'll be bound," she said. "Hiding away in some corner, likely. I didn't see her anywhere here when I came in, now I think on it. Maybe Betsy or her Tom took her back to their house to be out of my road. Good-bye, Lucy! Take good care of your mother and that little new bairn, mind!" and away she went.

As soon as she had gone I moved the bench across the door to keep it closed. I wondered how long it had been left open like that. I looked quickly in all the places where Sarah might be hiding in the kitchen, though I didn't think it likely she'd keep on hiding and not showing herself after she had heard me come in.

I hurried up the ladder. There was Mother asleep, and

there was the new babby all swaddled up, asleep as well. She was red and wrinkled and tiny, just as Sarah had been when she was newborn, but there was a difference somehow, as though this one's face had been made much more carefully. But I didn't like her any better than our Sarah, for all that. I looked all around the loft, under Mother and Father's bed and everywhere, but there was no sign of Sarah.

I durst not leave Mother and her new babby alone while I set out searching for Sarah, in spite of the candle and the breeches, but waiting for Father and Richard to come home was an uneasy time. There was plenty of work down in the kitchen that I could busy myself with. Betsy Greenwell or Janey or someone had taken the loaves out of the oven, but there was a deal of clearing up and putting away to do, and then I set about chopping vegetables to make broth, as there was only enough in the pot for Father when he came in off the fell, and more needed for next morning.

I was glad enough to hear Richard pushing at the door, and using words that no Puritan should have uttered at the clattering down of the bench when he clashed the door open. He knew nothing of what had been going on during the day, as he never came home for his dinner. He just took some maslin with him and ate it at midday in the archery field, where he went for target practice with the other lads. After school was finished he would stay wrestling and racing with them till dusk.

I hadn't finished the telling of it all before Richard was

up into the loft, giving me no time to warn him to be quiet. He said the babby was already whimpering when he got there, but I was fair taken aback when she set up such a yowling as you wouldn't believe could come from such a tiny creature. Richard said it was nothing as disagreeable as our Sarah used to sound when she was newborn, but I'd say it was six and two threes.

So I lifted her out of her cradle and gave her to my mother, who had been woken by the bellowing, and then there was peace again. I asked Mother where Sarah was, but her voice was that weak I couldn't make out what she was saying, and she looked so strange and ill that I durstn't worry her by more questionings. It seemed best to leave them quiet then, so we went down into the kitchen and I told Richard about Janey Foster not knowing where Sarah was, and asked if he had seen her anywhere outside. He just said "No" and shrugged his shoulders, so I asked would he go around to Betsy Greenwell's and see if she was there, and ask Betsy when she had last seen her if she wasn't. I'd have gone myself, but I thought it fitter for a girl to be minding my poor tired mother and her restless babby than a lad.

"I'm hungry," he said. "I'll have summat to eat afore I go seeking anyone!" I said he could take some cheese and bread with him to eat on the way, and I gave him what I hadn't eaten at Frosterley. He went off unwillingly enough, muttering that he would go to Betsy Greenwell's and no farther, for he wasn't for traipsing all over the county looking for a bairn such as Sarah.

Father came in before Richard was back. He took just one look at our mother and her new babby and told me to run to Janey Foster's quick as I could, and bring Janey straight back.

So I did that.

It wasn't often I had the chance to talk to them that had the second sight and knew about all the things that Janey knew about. So as we were hurrying back home again I asked her if, supposing a bairn were taken by the Little People, would there be any way at all that the family could get it back?

Janey was out of breath, so she slowed down for a moment before she spoke.

"That depends," she said. "It depends on which sort of bairn you mean—one of our human bairns, or one of Theirs. If one of ours were taken without being changed for one of Theirs, there's no way to get them back. There's them that tries, but I've never in my lifetime known of any that succeeded yet, and plenty that have come to grief trying. But if one of ours were changed for one of Theirs when they were both newborns, and the changeling were badly treated, They could take it back again, and it might be They'd return ours—if you were lucky! But don't you worry about that Sarah of yours. You've got a proper canny little lass now to care for."

Then she started scurrying along really fast to make up for the time she had lost talking, so I didn't question her anymore. I'd have liked her to think that I hadn't been asking about our Sarah specially—just any kind of bairn—but I'm not sure she would have believed me. Janey sometimes seemed to know what folk were thinking better than they knew theirselves.

When we got home, Richard was back in the kitchen, and there was no sign of Sarah. As soon as Janey Foster had gone up into the loft I asked him what Betsy had said about her. There was no comfort in his answer.

"She'd been far too busy with the birth, helping Janey Foster in all the commotion, to look where Sarah was and what she was doing. She said that if Sarah had gone missing, it were best for all of us to let her stay missing. And that," he added, "is the most sensible thing I ever heard that featherbrained Betsy Greenwell say."

It was more than an hour later that Father came down for his supper, leaving Janey in the loft, busying with Mother.

When we asked him how our mother was, he only said, "She's badly," and then sat on the cracket staring into the fire. Always a very silent man, our father was. He didn't eat much of his supper either, when it was set on the table, and never moved or spoke when Janey came down to brew some herbs on the fire.

At last, close on midnight it must have been, he went up again, though I doubt he went to bed up there. Janey had told Richard and me to keep out of the way, so we slept down there by the fire in the kitchen, the way our old Granny used to.

Soon after Father had gone up I thought I heard our cock crowing in the yard, but it seemed such an unlikely time to be doing that that I decided I must have dozed off to sleep and started dreaming.

There were such a lot of scratchy, scuttering noises down there in the kitchen that night, from mice and rats and crickets mostly, I suppose, without having to bear with Richard's snoring and grunting as well; outside there were owls, and a gusty wind.

A weary, restless night it was for all of us.

9

Vandals in the Church

Mother was shivering next morning. Shivering as though it were freezing cold, though she was hot like a fire with the fever she had, and when I spoke to her she didn't seem to understand what I was saying, or even to hear me.

Janey Foster, very quiet, which was quite unlike herself, was doing what had to be done for the babby. I asked her what was the matter with my mother, but she only whispered very softly so as not to disturb her, "I have done everything that could be done. But the cock crowed at midnight, did you not hear it?"

I remembered then that the day after we found Granny dead down there in the kitchen Charity Maddison had asked me if I had heard a cock crowing at midnight. I hadn't then, and thought it an unlikely thing to happen, but last night I had indeed heard one, and I wondered how the cocks knew what was going to happen, and if they were ever mistaken.

Father stayed at the bedside all that morning. I was up and down the ladder time and again, going down to see after the hens, milking the goat, fetching water from the well, seeing to the pot on the fire and all the things that have to be done from time to time, and at all times, come whatsoever, as well as doing whatever Janey asked me to do with that little new one up there in her cradle.

Once I asked Father what we were going to call the little one, but he just sat staring in front of him as though he hadn't heard me, and when I asked again he only shook his head.

Uncle William came in at dinnertime, having heard something of our trouble, for Betsy Greenwell had spread the news about in the village.

When he saw the way Mother was, and the strange taking my father was in too, he said he would see after our sheep along with his own, for they grazed together on the fell.

He told us there had been some Roundhead soldiers drinking in the alehouse that morning. All but two were strangers making their way south, home to Yorkshire, sleeping in what shelter they could find. They had been up as far as Dunbar with Cromwell's army, where there had been a great victory over the Scots a month before, the time the Scots were fighting on the Royalist side, trying to bring the young prince Charles on to the English throne. Uncle William had wondered how they could pay for the amount of drink they were taking, for Roundheads would be offered scant hospitality in our village.

I told my uncle about Sarah being lost, and he said he would keep his eyes open for her, and if he saw her he would keep her by him till he could get her home to us. If he didn't find her by that evening he'd have the crier call out for her on the next market day. He would have it called out in Stanhope, and in Bishops Aukland, too, if need be, that she was lost. I was glad for someone else to be trying to find Sarah beside myself. My uncle William was a very kind man.

After he had gone I set everything to rights down in the kitchen, moving about on tiptoe and trying not to clatter. It was very, very quiet up above. So quiet that I became anxious and climbed stealthily up the ladder to see what was doing in the loft chamber. Father, staring blankly beside the big bed, was the only one awake. I don't think he noticed me. Janey Foster, who had been up and busy all night, was, no wonder, drooped on our bed, sound asleep from exhaustion. Mother was so pale and so deathly still it frightened me, but she must have only been sleeping, else Father would have surely wakened Janey. The bairn in the cradle with the breeches alongside was peacefully asleep as well.

I crept back down the ladder without saying anything.

I kept as quiet as I could, thinking of what Granny used to say about sleeping, and hoping they were all sleeping themselves better up there. But I didn't know whether you'd say my mother were a young un or an old un—that was the trouble—she didn't really seem to be one or the other at that time.

There seemed to be nothing left to do down there but the spinning and knitting that were always there for the doing from one shearing to the next. If I slipped away for a little while I might well not be missed, not till Janey woke, anyway. I decided to risk it.

I would run fast as I could to the churchyard and the riverside, her two favorite places, just to satisfy myself that Sarah was not there before I asked anyone else about her. Minnie Ward would be the last person I would ask, but it might have to be even her.

I crept quietly out of the house. Father must have mended the house door while I was fetching Janey. I closed it gently behind me and ran down the street as fast as I could, thankful that it was empty, else people would have kept stopping me to ask how my mother was, and I had no time to spare for answering.

When I turned up Church Lane I could see four or five people ahead of me, hurrying toward the church. I ran on, to find that there was quite a gathering of folk in the churchyard, which was well trampled. They were clustered around the porch mostly, and a chattering and waving of arms going on, with a few fists shaken as well.

A young soldier was barring the closed door of the church with his pike. He was not so much a man as a tall, freckled boy, such as our Richard might have been if they had cropped his hair shorter and fitted him out as a soldier. I guessed he must be one of the Roundhead soldiers that Uncle William had seen in the alehouse. Then, when the sound of crashes and blows and tinkling stone coming from inside the church was met by angry shouts from the villagers outside, I guessed what must be happening in there.

Two young women tried to push past the soldier's pike, but it was no use. The young man stood his ground, firmly and silently.

Then a cry went up of "Where is the priest?" and "Fetch the priest!" but just at that moment the church door was flung open from inside and about a dozen men came tumbling out. They were an odd mingle of soldiers and villagers, some with pikes or muskets and some with hammers or axes. I recognized Hugh Trotter and Thomas Wooler; both were Puritans who had left Wulsingham some weeks before to join the army.

Till that time I had always thought of Puritans as very serious and sober men. And, indeed, most of the Puritans I have known since that time were such. But these men, with the exception of the young guard outside, were very far from being sober.

Often enough the smashing of ornaments by Cromwell's soldiers in the churches of towns and villages as they passed through them was put down to religious zeal. Yet I felt sure that the zeal of these stragglers drifting home from the battlefield was prompted more by ale than religious conviction.

The crowd was in an angry mood when the sexton arrived with the great key to lock the door, which would have had reason had he locked it before the damage had been done. But how was he to know? Someone said the priest was away giving the sacrament to a sick woman in one of the outlying farms.

Those who had been in the church made away in all different directions. Some of our lads gave chase, but whether they caught any of them and what happened to the culprits if they did, I didn't wait to find out. There was no sign of Sarah in that noisy, jostling crowd, and it was Sarah that I was seeking, and Sarah that concerned me most. I did wonder, though, just what had happened in the church there, and whether our little stone dollies had been hurt. I was too anxious to get back to Mother and be home before I was missed to wait my chance to slip into the church and see how Sir John and his family had fared.

I took the river path, running as fast as I could, but looking all the time for Sarah as I went—the second time I had run along that path in panic looking for her.

When I got back to our cottage Richard was alone in the kitchen. It was he who told me that Mother was dead.

10

The New Sarah

I could not believe that the new babby was really going to be christened Sarah. Father said that unless that other were back home before we set off to the church, then Sarah would be her name, for such had been her mother's dying wish, and dying wishes should always be respected.

"But why?" I asked. "Why did she want 'Sarah' when we already have a Sarah in our family?"

My father shook his head.

"Not now, we haven't," he said. "It seems she's gone. Maybe she wasn't ever rightly in our family at all; maybe she were a stranger, brought in from outside. It could be that this one in the cradle was really Sarah, near six year ago, and was taken away, and brought back, like."

I felt angry hearing it from my own father. It was bad enough when the neighbors were hinting and winking and nodding. It was worse still to think that even our mother may have believed it at the end. She must at least have thought that Sarah was alive somewhere and not coming back, for if she were dead, she wouldn't have dared to use her name again. Everyone in these parts knows that disaster follows from naming a child after a dead brother or sister; and there are enough disasters without tempting them that way.

Yet if they believed that about Mother's first Sarah being brought back by the Little People, then where was the new babby that Mother had just had? There should have been two in the cradle then, shouldn't there? Or had they taken her as well, in spite of the candle and the breeches? The more I tried to work it out, the more mixed up I became.

"You don't mean that our Sarah was a . . . ?" The word stuck in my throat. I don't think "changeling" was a forbidden word, even in those days, not like "fairies" was. But I couldn't bring myself to say it out loud, for I had always been so determined that our Sarah wasn't one.

"A man is sometimes hard put to know what to think" was all my father said.

Uncle William rode over to Frosterley that evening to fetch our Martha home for the funeral and the christening.

I was glad to have her home for the christening, for if she hadn't been there, they'd have had me carry the new Sarah myself, and I was told that that would have been a great honor for me, but I didn't want to do it. I turned my head away and wished I could shut my ears when the priest was giving our Sarah's name to that new babby. It seemed like he was stealing, and I would have liked to have nothing to do with it.

Turning my back on the ceremony and twisting my head around as much as I dared, I could see something of the damage that had been done by the soldiers. Sir John's nose and a piece of his hand had been chipped right off, and though they were only such small pieces of alabaster, they were enough to take away all his pride and dignity. I would never be so afraid of him again, I was sure, looking the way he did then.

The rampage had evidently not disturbed Lady Catherine. She slept on, serene as ever, without a scratch on her gentle face; but the little children were all badly knocked about and battered. As for the Sarah-dolly, from where I stood it looked as though there was only a space at the end of the line where she should have been.

As soon as the service was finished, the congregation crowded around our Martha and the new Sarah in the churchyard, twittering and admiring, saying what a good, sweet, quiet bairn she was, only yowling when the holy water fell on her. That was always reckoned to be a lucky sign, for bairns that didn't cry at the sprinkling were believed to be over-good to live.

I slipped away from all the smiling and nodding and babbling and ran back into the church and up to Sir John's table. The little dollies underneath it, scratched and chipped, had suffered even more than I had feared. Several arms had been knocked off, and the Sarah-dolly was gone. There was only a sort of stump where she had been, like what is left of a tree that has been felled. It would have broken Sarah's heart to see it the way it was. I looked on the floor and all around to see if there was any trace of her, or any of the others, but there was not a chip to be seen anywhere.

I went home by myself, the long way around. I didn't want to be with Father and Martha and Richard and the new Sarah just then—especially the new Sarah. I wanted to be with Mother and our first Sarah. I couldn't believe that I wouldn't see either of them ever again, even though I had seen Mother's coffin put into the earth two days before. As for Sarah, I kept telling myself that she was only hiding somewhere. She always did love hiding, that one.

After the funeral and the christening were over, there was talk of Martha leaving the Turnbulls' and stopping home for good.

Mistress Charlton and Betsy Greenwell were in our cottage a lot at that time, giving a hand with this and that, and telling me how best to help, and showing me how to do things that my mother had taught me how to do long since—but all very kindly meant, I don't doubt.

In the evening, when Martha was outside shutting up the hens and I was in the loft chamber seeing to the new Sarah, I could hear their chattering floating up through the ladderhole and the floorboards.

They thought that with two grown men to feed (for Richard was a big man in appetite, for all he was still at school) and that babby to care for (even though she were such a little good un; not like that other freak, thank goodness, and what a blessing that one had been "taken back," and how much easier it would be for all of us without her), it needed more than an eleven-year-old bit of a lass to keep the home working. They thought that Joseph Emerson (that was my father's name) would be a fool not to keep Martha home now she were here, she being such a strong, hard-working lass. Though it were a good place she had at the Turnbulls by all accounts. Still, the Turnbulls were Roundheads, more's the pity.

Then, when they had said it all, they said it all again, such chatterers they were!

When we were in bed that same evening, I told Martha the most of what I had heard them saying.

She jerked angrily under the bedclothes.

"I told Father I'd be going back tomorrow, and he said nowt about staying on here," she complained. "It's a busy time on the farm just now, and they'll be needing me."

I might have said it was a busy time here at home, too, and always was, as far as I could tell, but I didn't.

We lay quiet for a time, and then, more calmly, she said, "What do you think has happened to Sarah?"

"How could I know what has happened to her?" I said. "Tom Greenwell forced the door open and hadn't the sense to make it fast again, so she toddled off and disappeared, such as any bairn might when it gets the chance. I've looked for her and Uncle William's looked for her, and the crier's called for her in three different markets. If anyone'd seen her, she'd have been fetched back."

"Then do you think she's been taken?" Martha said.

"Taken? Taken where?" I asked. "There's been no faws or tinkers nor any such round hereabouts, not for long enough."

"I wasn't meaning the faws," she said.

"You mean the Little People?"

"Who else would I mean? Who else would want a bairn like that?"

"But Sarah isn't a bairn like that! She wasn't—I mean isn't—one of Them! She's a proper human child, Sarah is!"

Then, surprisingly gentle, Martha said, "It will be a great deal easier for you, Lucy, and all of us, with her gone."

I suppose she was trying to be kind, knowing how fond I was of Sarah, but it wasn't what I wanted her to say.

After that Martha didn't want to talk about it anymore. She shut her eyes and pretended to be asleep. I stayed awake for a long time, trying to keep out of the way of her fidgety legs. At least it was a little easier in bed with only the two of us. Easier, but not happier.

In the morning I woke before it was light, to find myself alone in our bed. Martha had gone. She must have gathered her things together and left the house very quietly not to have woken any of us.

I wondered why she had been in such a hurry to get back to the Turnbull farm, setting off that long way by herself before daybreak, on foot. There must have been something or someone she was very fond of about that place.

11

A New Mother

For the next two years I had to look after that new Sarah almost as though I were a grown woman and she were my daughter, not my sister: washing her and feeding her, and seeing to her clothes as she grew out of them, and everything; work that I enjoyed much more than scrubbing and cleaning and polishing, I must say. If that had been the only work, I would have been happy enough, for she was a good bairn, and I reckon she didn't make a quarter of the mess that the other Sarah used to make, and that had never troubled me. But the scrubbing and cleaning and polishing was all to be done at the same time, as well as keeping the family and the animals fed, week in, week out, so that most days I used to be all but asleep standing up long before bedtime.

Yet, for all she was so good (though not *always* the "regular little lady" that the neighbors kept telling me she was) I was never fond of her in the same way I used to be fond of the first Sarah. There seemed to be a sort of fence between us, and I expect that fence was my lost Sarah.

She never laughed at the same things that used to amuse Sarah, although she laughed plenty. She never had the hiccups that I can remember, nor would she have thought it funny if she had. And, except when she was a very tiny babby, she never burped, and then not in the boisterous way that Sarah always enjoyed. She was dainty and sweet, like a very pretty, tow-haired doll; a doll for keeping in a box, not for playing with. Leastways not the way Sarah and I used to play with our dollies.

Richard finished with school soon after Mother died, so he was busy helping Father, doing most of the work that Martha and I used to do together, as well as real heavy man's work. He grumbled a great deal at the war's finishing. Father insisted that there was no call for him to be joining the militia when there was more than enough to keep him occupied on our plot. If it had been the Royalists Richard was so ready to fight for, maybe Father wouldn't have been so strict about stopping him. I don't know.

Neighbors were very kind, though, always in and out to see if I were managing all right, and giving a hand, lots of ways, though sometimes our kitchen was that full of kindly folk and their wise advice that I thought I could manage quicker without a few of them.

One that I could certainly have done better without was that Hetty Bell. Quite a young woman she was, not that much older than our Martha, with a loud, shrill voice. She was on our doorstep more than any of them, bringing in pies and tatie-cake and sweetmeats she had made for "the poor lonely man" or "the poor motherless bairn" — and that always meant the new Sarah, not me. Always walking past Richard and me as though we weren't even there. When she was in the house, how we wished we weren't!

With my father being such a quiet, shy sort of man, it didn't surprise me that he used to keep out of the house and out of the way of Hetty Bell whenever he heard her piercing prattle coming from the kitchen. I used to keep out of her way myself as much as I could. But often enough she would go out into the byre to seek him. We could hear her right across the yard, telling him what she had brought and how tasty it was. Charity Maddison heard her giving tongue one time and said it was like sounding a trumpet before her, the way it says in the Bible you shouldn't do. Except that Hetty's voice was far worse nor any trumpet.

In all that time I never once stopped looking for Sarah. Every time I stepped out of the house I had a tiny candle of hope in me that I might see her hiding behind some gate or tree or wall. Of course as weeks went by I knew it was less and less likely she could still be alive somewhere, and maybe the looking and hoping just became a habit, but I never gave it up. No one ever spoke of her in Wulsingham anymore.

Things happen so gradually sometimes that you don't realize what's going on till one day you shake yourself awake and come to your senses. Then you wonder how you can have been blind for so long. That was the way it happened about Father and Hetty Bell.

I mentioned it to Richard the same evening as I woke up to what was going on, asking if he had noticed the way Hetty was spending more and more time in our home and less and less time with her old mother, who was a widow and crippled and might well have done with a bit of Hetty's help herself.

Richard only laughed and said he wasn't blind, and he wasn't deaf neither, though that were a wonder with that screech-mouth filling the place with her noise the way she did.

"Have you noticed the way Father seems not to mind her now?" I asked.

Richard nodded, scowling. "Everyone in Wulsingham noticed, long since," he said, "excepting you, and everyone knows where it is leading. Finding the way to a man's heart through his stomach, that's all. Not for the first time, neither. It's bin done before!"

He went out into the yard, clashing the door behind him.

It was only a few weeks after that that Father told me we were going to have a new mother. Hetty Bell had consented to marry him. She wouldn't have taken much persuading either, I'll be bound.

He said how good it would be for me to have her sharing the housework, and looking after me and the new Sarah. He couldn't think of anything to say after that. He was always a man of few words. Nor could I think of anything to say neither — not to him I couldn't — being fond of him and not wanting to hurt his feelings. I didn't know how I was going to make myself agreeable to Hetty Bell, or even what I was supposed to call her. "Step-mother" I should think; I wouldn't call her "Mother," that I did know. I didn't want to ask Father about it. I couldn't even think of her as anybody's mother, let alone mine. It was different for the new Sarah. She had never called anyone else "Mother," so she wouldn't have any feelings that way.

It was horrid hearing the banns called in church. I wanted to put my hands over my ears. I stared straight in front of me so as to avoid seeing the looks of pity or I-told-you-so that I imagined there would be on the faces of the congregation, and I felt my face turning red with shame.

I used to like going to church with the family when Mother and our Sarah and the little Sarah-dolly and all her brothers and sisters were there. Now that they had gone, and there had been Mother's funeral and the new Sarah's hateful christening in it, I didn't want to go to church anymore, but of course I had to go, the same as everyone else. Then the thought of that wedding being in the church made it seem a really evil place to me.

A week before Father's marriage to Hetty my mind was made up. I would not live day and night in the same house as Hetty Bell. If nothing would stop her coming, then I would have to go.

12

In Search of Fairies

It was clear to me that I had to run away, but where to run was not so clear. I had never been out of the dale, nor ever farther up it than the Turnbull farm above Frosterley, and it would have been no use going to that farm, where I'd have been sent straight back home, I don't doubt. As soon as I had left home they'd have the crier calling for me, the same as they did for Sarah, and I would have to go far and quickly to be out of reach.

Yet they never found Sarah for all the crier's crying. If only I had known how she got away so suddenly and completely, I could have followed her, wheresoever it was—to Heaven or Hell or fairy caves. I didn't really think it was the Little People had taken her, but if it wasn't Them, then where was she? If she were in Heaven or Hell, she'd have left her body behind somewhere, wouldn't she?

The more I thought about Sarah being in some strange place, the more I wanted to be with her, looking after her, and far away from Hetty Bell. Maybe spying on the Little People would bring trouble on me, I've heard that often enough, but wasn't trouble on me anyway? If I went to a fairy cave I might find Sarah, or leastways hear some news of her.

The only fairy caves I had ever seen were those tiny ones close by Frosterley that were far too little even for Sarah to creep inside, the size she was when we last saw her. But maybe I could call into them, or catch a sight of the Nameless Ones as they darted in and out, and perhaps learn something of her whereabouts. I had heard that the milkmaids had sighted Them dancing near Clints Crags, where there are dark green rings on the grass such as there always are where the Little People have held their revels. But I didn't know where Clints Crags was, nor how to get there.

I made up my mind to go to the Frosterley caves the very next time that Hetty Bell came to our house. I didn't have to wait long. She was an early caller, so soon after breakfast my chance came. It wasn't hard to slip out and around to the front of the house while Hetty was prattling away to Father in the kitchen and Richard was mending fences around the back.

I didn't go through Wulsingham along the Frosterly road because there would be too many inquisitive folk wondering where I was going so fast along that way, but I turned down to the river. I knew our river was the same river they had at Frosterley, so if I followed along it, I could but get there.

It was not so easy as I thought it would be, though. There was a trod by the water's edge some parts, but not all the way, and there were sudden boggy places and thick bushes to push past, and sometimes it was quicker going along the riverbed itself where the river was running shallow with wide stony beaches at its edges, but never very quick on those big round stones, neither.

I passed a tumbledown hovel that once must have been Minnie Ward's cottage. Nearly two years ago Minnie had gone from Wulsingham, no one knew where; no one except, perhaps, an old body still alive at that time, whose name I have forgotten. She must have been about the last of the ancient women in our village who used to consult the old fraud about their ailments. I was thankful then that I had never had quite enough courage to ask Minnie's advice about Sarah till it was too late, for I didn't believe that any of her faked magic charms would have brought her back to me, even if she had been taken by the Little People.

At last I was able to see the roofs of Frosterley up to the right there, so I left the river and went straight toward them, crossing the road before I got into the village. I didn't want folks staring at me the way they do, so I went around the backs of the houses for fear of meeting that old woman, or anyone else, and I found the place easily enough.

I didn't hear any singing this time, though; no piping or fiddling or anything at all when I put my ear to the grass. Certainly no grasshoppers or bumlers either.

I crept up quietly to the opening of the little cave. Of course I wouldn't be able to get inside it, but perhaps if I put my ear against it I maybe could hear something going on in there. But I didn't. The only sound was the burn hurrying down the hill. Perhaps if I put my hand right inside I might feel something, but I was rather frightened—what might Little People not do to it if they found a great mortal hand pushing down into their kingdom?

I was just stretching my hand out toward it when a shadow fell on it. I looked up, startled, and recognized from my earlier visit, young Roger Turnbull!

"Looking for fairies?" he asked as though it were a perfectly ordinary thing to say.

"You shouldn't name them!" I said. "You really shouldn't!" and then I remembered Martha saying how the Turnbulls didn't believe in any such, and I felt awkward and ashamed to be looking for what didn't exist for him, for he was older than me, and all but a grown man. Though I really had no call to feel ashamed about it when everyone else I knew except the Turnbulls believed in Them at that time, and there's plenty still do to this day.

Roger smiled. "I forgot," he said simply. "Are you looking for the Nameless Ones?"

I nodded. "I think perhaps our Sarah is with Them," I said.

It was a foolish thing to say to him if he truly didn't believe there were Nameless Ones or Little People or fairies or any such, call Them what you will. But he looked so kindly that I went on to tell him how I had always been looking for my little sister whenever I had the chance, these two year gone. So seeing he seemed interested and really listening I threw all prudence to the winds and went on to tell him that now I was going to look for Sarah all the time without stopping till I found her—for the rest of my life, if need be, because I had left Wulsingham forever, as nothing could be worse than being at home when Hetty Bell became Hetty Emerson.

Now, if I wanted to run away and not be found, you might rightly say that there was nothing sillier I could do than confide in young Roger Turnbull, seeing how Martha was working at the Turnbull farm and there was nothing simpler for them to do than send me back to where I belonged, to a scolding or worse from Hetty and sad, reproachful looks from my father, I don't doubt; and that only the beginning of it.

But Roger said nothing of sending me home. All he said was, "It's no use looking in there, Lucy. There's none in there now, even if there ever were. I've heard that the priest exorcised the fair—the Nameless Ones a year ago, set them adrift the way they did the ones from Clint Crags. Some say the Clint Crags ones flitted to caves at Westerhope, but there's no saying where these have gone. You'd best come back to our farm with me and have a gossip with your Martha while you're so near. Then maybe have something to eat and a bit sup while you're about it."

So that is what I did. While I was having a good meal with our Martha, talking some but listening more, mostly about how well she thought of Roger Turnbull, Roger was at the back of the house with his parents, his younger brothers and his sister. A thorough family talking must have been going on among them. Then, some long while afterward, in came old John Turnbull and said that seeing his wife's rheumatism was plaguing her more every winter, and as they were so satisfied with our Martha, and me not happy at home anymore, maybe I would like to go and live with them, helping alongside Martha. I was younger than she was when she started there, yet I had been doing a grown woman's work at home ever since my mother died. And if, after a trial, both I and they were satisfied, I'd have an annual wage as well as my keep, same as any other young woman in place.

That all sounded fine enough till Mistress Turnbull came in and said they'd have to have my father's consent before anything was settled, and that my father must be told at once where I was. Letting my father know where I was was the very thing I had been trying to avoid. So that was when I began to feel really uneasy, because what suited me and the Turnbulls might not suit him. And how would Hetty Bell feel about losing a pair of hands, even a pair as small as mine were, that were useful for cleaning and cooking and milking and looking after our new Sarah?

I think John Turnbull must have guessed what I was

thinking, for he said he would ride over to Wulsingham that very afternoon to put my father's mind at rest concerning my whereabouts, and perhaps come to some agreement about the future, but for that night at least, I'd be sleeping with Martha again.

As soon as he had gone, Martha whispered to me that John Turnbull had quite an uncanny way of talking people around to his own way of thinking. I only hoped she was right.

It was late in the evening before he came back, carrying a big bundle that was wrapped in one of our bedcovers.

"Can I stay?" I asked as soon as he had set foot in the kitchen. "Is it all right?"

He laughed, and paused deliberately before answering, amused at my impatience. "Aye, Lucy, you can stay," he said. "Everything has been discussed and settled. What a kind, gentle man your father is! He asked me to tell you, most particularly, that he wished you well and would look forward to seeing both you and Martha next quarter day, which will be a holiday."

He made no mention of Hetty Bell. Perhaps she was too busy with preparation for the wedding to give full heed to what was being said, or maybe she thought she would get a greater share of my father's attention if I were out of the road. I guessed she didn't care for me any more than I did for her.

He handed me the bundle; all my clothes were in it, as

well as a brooch of which I was particularly fond, which had once belonged to my mother.

So that was how I came to be in place at the Turnbulls. A fine place it was to be in, too, for though the work was hard, and Mistress Turnbull as strict as anyone I've met before or since, she was kindhearted with it as all those Turnbulls were. Neither did I lack anything in the way of good food or good company. One thing only was missing for me, and that was our Sarah.

13

News at Last

I was very happy growing up as one of the family at the Turnbulls, working on the farm and in the kitchen alongside our Martha and Prudence Turnbull. The three of us slept in the loft over the byre, but I had a little pallet all to myself, so I was out of the way of Martha's restless legs, for which I was thankful.

I learned to read and write at that time, which suited me just as well as, or even better than going to school would have done. John Turnbull was a real good scholar as well as a good farmer, and he said he would make a scholar of me if I really wanted to read and was willing to work hard. So in the winter evenings, when I had worked well all day, he would take me into the parlor and teach me my letters so that I was soon able to spell out some of the words in the big Bible that he had. That Bible was the first book I had ever seen that was in an ordinary person's house, not in a church. If it wasn't for the master starting me on my letters and allowing me to read the books he had, I'd never have been writing this story now.

Several years passed without even the briefest visits home (because of Hetty). Martha's courting days were over. She had married young Roger Turnbull and they had left us to live in a tiny cottage belonging to the farm, half a mile farther up the fell. Roger still worked for his father on the farm, but they had a small patch of land of their own as well. So what with looking after Roger, and growing vegetables, and the goats and hens that they had, and a baby on the way before long, Martha could not give us much help.

Mistress Turnbull was delighted at the prospect of another grandchild, for she had only half a dozen, but she sorely missed Martha's muscles and willing service. Prudence and I together couldn't get through what the three of us used to do, try as we did. So there was soon talk of hiring another girl.

It was after the master had been up to Stanhope market one day that he came home saying how he had been talking after the sales to an elderly cousin of his, a shepherd from Cudderstane way, in Teesdale. This cousin was a neighbor of a large family of Watsons, mostly lasses, and seemingly there was some difficulty getting the third one placed round about where they lived. The farmers there must have had plenty daughters of their own just at that particular time. Turnbull's cousin was pleased to put in a word for Marion, as they called her. She was a handy sort of lass for indoors or out, and from all he knew of her family, she would surely be a good, honest, hard worker.

So it came about that a week after that, Marion was settled in at the Turnbull farm, helping with the butter making and cheese making and the hay and the scrubbing, and sleeping in the loft with Prudence and me.

I had never before heard anyone talk the way that Marion Watson talked. On and on she went, whatever she was doing, much more, even, than Hetty Bell, though not loud and angry like Hetty, more like a sort of buzzing of bees at swarming time, without any stopping for breath at all.

She always talked as though you knew all the people she was telling you about as well as she knew them herself, as if you knew whether Thomas or Henry or Joseph was a brother or cousin or a neighbor or just a stranger she had met at the fair, and not a pause in the buzzing for you to ask the question and find out, neither.

After the first few days I didn't listen all that carefully to what she was saying and stopped trying to puzzle out who all the people were — there were that many of them. I just listened with one ear to Marion, keeping the other open for Mistress Turnbull's orders, and the clock's chiming, and the lark's singing and all else that I used to listen to before she came. It was easier that way, and after half listening for a few weeks I gradually came to know something, though certainly not everything, of her family and friends and their life in Teesdale. At night, though, I had to pull the covers up over both my ears to shut out the chatter or else I would have had to finish with sleeping altogether. Prudence slept through a thunderstorm once, so she didn't mind.

About three months after Marion came, when we were turning the hay together one afternoon, she was chattering away about something or other, and me wondering all the time about my little sister, as I so often did, wondering where she was and what she was doing, so that I was paying even less attention to Marion than I sometimes did, when I half heard her say something about "that daft little Sarah."

Now, if I had stopped to listen for just one minute, giving myself time to separate my own thoughts from Marion's babble, I've no doubt I'd have spoken differently. But I didn't. I just snapped out, "But our Sarah isn't daft! Leastways, not so daft as most make out!"

"Calm yoursel' down, Lucy!" Marion laughed. "You'd know if you'd been listening that I weren't talking about *your* Sarah. I never knew you even had a one called Sarah. I were talking about that silly little girl our Henry found lost and sickening on the fell when he were coming back from the wars. *She* were daft all right!"

I listened then carefully enough, with both ears. For surely it was just as the soldiers were coming home from the war that our Sarah disappeared from Wulsingham.

It was a long story the way Marion told it. Her stories always were long ones, and there was plenty in them that had to do with Marion's opinions and little enough to do with the parts of the story I was wanting to hear. I bit my lips hard so as not to interrupt her, not even when she said that about the little daft girl being so foolish-fond of some plaything she called her "Sarah-dolly." I heard her right out to what seemed to be the end, and then I knew for certain it was our Sarah she had been talking about.

"But what happened to her?" I had to ask when she at last came to a stop. "Where is she now?"

"I dunno," she said. "Dead, likely."

Then off she rattled into another chapter of the most confused story I had ever heard her tell, and at such a rate I can't say how she found the breath to do it. Yet among all the muddle of it there kept coming up odd things which I recognized as so characteristic of Sarah that there could be no doubt whom she was talking about. Even if I could have slowed her down and written all she said as from a dictation, I still think no one could have unraveled her story.

It was not till later, after I had met her brother Henry, that I learned all the truth of it, but at least I knew now that Sarah had reached Teesdale, and that Marion had seen her more recently than I had.

So then I told Marion about our Sarah—the way she looked, and the size of her, and the gown she was wearing when she was lost, and everything, and that there were some who said she was daft, though my mother had never called her daft, and she'd have been the one to know if anyone did. Then I told about Sarah going missing at the time of the war's ending, and the way some said the Little People must have fetched her away, and how I didn't really believe that myself, but I didn't know what else to believe, neither.

Marion had stopped talking and listened, for maybe the longest time she had listened in all her life. She really seemed to think we had both been talking about the same little lass, and she said she was sorry for saying that Sarah was daft and stupid and dirty, because she didn't know she was my sister, or she'd have chosen her words more carefully. But I didn't care what words she had used about her if only she could help me find her again.

"Why don't you come home with me next quarter day and see our Henry; then he can tell you more than what I can, so you'll know for certain it were your sister that he found?"

I would have liked fine to go to Teesdale with Marion, but I didn't have to wait for quarter day to meet her brother Henry, because two weeks later it was Marion's birthday and he came riding over with gifts and good wishes from her family, which I thought kind of them, seeing they were a big family with plenty of birthdays coming up through the year.

Henry seemed to me to be the plain opposite of Marion. Where she was golden and curly and pink, he was dark and straight and burned brown from the sun. He was slow-spoken too, and quiet, with a kind, serious face. But when Marion told him that we guessed I was his Sarah's sister (strangely enough I hardly minded when she called her "his Sarah"), his face woke up and he was so excited he could scarce find the words to ask all the questions he wanted answering. It was me that had the flow of words for all the questions I wanted answering by him. It was soon plain without any possible doubt that it really was our Sarah that he had rescued from exhaustion on the fell there, some six years before. There and then he set to and told me the whole story.

14

The Beginning of Henry Watson's Story

So here is the story of how Henry Watson came across our Sarah on Bollyop Fell. I will tell it, so near as I can remember, just as he told it to me that afternoon, except, of course, that he didn't tell it fully and in the right order the first time, with me too impatient not to interrupt with questions all along and hurrying him on to tell the ending before he had got to the middle; and some small things he didn't think to tell till long afterward. But he always spoke clearly and slowly enough to be followed without any difficulty, and never contradicted himself or got tied up in knots the way Marion did with her stories. Except that I've written "he" or "Henry" where he said "I," it is pieced together with the very words he used in his telling, for as I write I find I can remember his talk as though it were yesterday instead of all those years ago.

It was back in 1650 just after he had been up into Scotland at the Battle of Dunbar, where Cromwell's army had such a victory over the Scots, the Scots who were fighting to put Prince Charles onto the English throne after his father had been beheaded.

Henry was one of the infantry men who had marched the six thousand Scottish prisoners into England, though only three thousand survived by the time they reached Durham, for food was not easily come by even for the guards when every mouthful had to be forcibly taken, for it was mostly Royalist country that they were passing through.

At Durham his military duty ended and he had the good fortune to acquire a horse. In an alehouse he met a near neighbor of his, Hobby Collinson, who had been dawdling home to Teesdale. Hobby had been in the cavalry, his father's good horse Jess being taken into service the same time that Hobby was. Hobby had heard a rumor that the prisoners were to be shipped eventually to the West Indies, and had set his heart on going with them in the capacity of a guard, and so fulfilling a childhood ambition to run away to sea, but confessed to a guilty feeling about selling the horse, which was not his to sell and was no doubt sorely missed on the farm.

Henry willingly agreed to return Jess to the Collinson farm at Cudderstane. Most of the rest of the infantrymen were moving south to Darnton, but Henry, who had offered to help a crippled companion to his home in Wulsingham, took the longer route to Teesdale through Weredale, the horse's four legs more than making up for the shorter distance it would have been on his own two.

He must have arrived in Wulsingham soon after the

soldiers who had been despoiling the parish church had left, for the village people were all talking about the damage that had been done and the shame of it.

Having taken his friend safely home to his family, Henry took a shortcut back to the road through the trampled churchyard. He came across a little heap of broken figures, heads of cherubs, the hands of a saint, and pieces of a stone garland hidden in the long grass beside a gravestone where the scythe had not reached. Cromwell's soldiers often gathered up "keepsakes" such as these which they sometimes sold. Perhaps they had been gathered together and then abandoned when their collector had had to beat a hasty retreat before the angry mob. Henry picked out a tiny but almost complete sculptured child, a doll it could be for one of his little sisters. Of course, as soon as Henry told me this I knew where it came from.

With the little figure in his pouch he turned Jess towards Bollyop Fell, beyond which lay Teesdale and home.

The weather was in his favor, a fair, dry day, but with the chill of autumn already in the air. He knew it could be a perilous, steep journey across that rough Pennine moorland in darkness or poor weather, but while the sun shone his heart was light at the thought of home ahead. Jess, who had been driven hard ever since they had left Durham early that morning, seemed to gather fresh strength, almost as though she understood that with each step she took she left the turmoil of the last few months behind her and was brought nearer to the peaceful fields of home. Henry let her make her own pace as they went up and away from the farms and cottages of the valley bottom, till they were in sight of nothing but ling and peat hags, blue sky and bright clouds. Once an adder slithered across their path just inches ahead of the horse's hooves and vanished into the ling on the other side, but Jess just plodded on steadily.

After they had gained a good height, Henry noticed the clouds blurring and lowering, and half an hour later they ran into a mist. At the same time their stony road narrowed so that Jess had to pick her way cautiously along it. As they went forward, so the mist thickened and it was soon hard to see the way ahead.

Henry's high spirits sank a little at the prospect of struggling across that lonely moor. He minded well how hazardous it might be in bad weather; apart from bog and crevasse lying in wait for a traveling stranger, there could be other dangers. There were, some said, evil spirits abroad on those high fells that divided Weredale from Teesdale, demons that the archangel Michael had thrust out of Heaven with that old serpent Satan, long, long ago. They had landed on lonely moorland such as this place was, and had lived on in the shape of imps or brown men or duergars. They guarded their territory jealously, hating humans who interfered with them, and doing nothing but harm.

Of course, like many another Puritan soldier, Henry set little store by such tales. They were all part of the old papist superstition, to his way of thinking, stories he had heard as a child but no longer believed. Yet he knew his Bible well and had heard the minister read of the archangel Michael from the Book of Revelation, and, he argued with himself, those wicked spirits must have dropped to somewhere on the earth when they fell out of the sky, and who was to say that the place was not Bollyop? He knew that old Satan himself fell into a bramble bush at that time, for didn't he spit for revenge on all the brambles every year on Michaelmas Day so folk cannot eat them after? So it would be likely that they all fell together at no great distance from Teesdale, or else how could his spit reach all the way to those brambles so near to their farm at Cudderstane? They never were fit for eating after Michaelmas. And if those demons did not turn into imps and duergars, what did become of them, then?

He tried to drive such gloomy thoughts from his mind by a singing of psalms and hymns which helped him through the monotony of that gray, drizzling twilight.

He had almost recovered his good humor when Jess shied at something white not far from the path and stopped suddenly.

"Come on, Jess lass," he coaxed, "move on now!"

Peering into the mist, he could not make out the form that had startled her. He tried to move her nearer to it, but Jess would neither move toward it nor continue along the path.

Jumping down, and pulling Jess unwillingly behind him by her bridle, he moved a little nearer to the whiteness and was startled to find it to be a white cap worn by a misshapen little creature in a brown cloak who was slumped against a stone, half sitting, half lying. Its face and hands were blue, and its far-apart eyes were closed, but whether in sleep or in death, he could not tell.

He moved near enough to see and hear that it was breathing. Was that what duergars looked like, then? He thought that if that was what it was, it would have been wiser to mount his horse and get away before it did him a mischief. But going closer still, he could see that beneath the brown cloak it was wearing a coarse linen gown, the same as an ordinary little mortal lass would wear. Imps or brown men or duergars would be breeched, wouldn't they? So could it have been a fairy? But it was too big for a fairy, leastways it wouldn't have fitted into the fairy cupboards down by the river at Cudderstane, where they say the Little People live, not by a long way.

It shifted in its sleep. It was breathing very snuffly, with a rattle in its chest that reminded him of something. That was just the way that poor bairn from neighbor Collinson's farm used to sound, that crippled one who had died the year before, when she was five year old. She was a harmless little thing by intent, but she was a deal of trouble to bring up, having such useless legs and not much understanding. There were even some that said she wasn't mortal either, but a changeling child. He thought that this one certainly sounded like that one, but that one hadn't a blue face or a crooked back humping up to its shoulders like this one. It could be the cold making it blue, though. Any human could have a blue face, lying out there on the ling in the mist for long enough. She could have been lying out there for hours, or even days, for all he knew.

But if she were a human, how she came to be there alone on the felltop Henry could only wonder. Later there were those that guessed the Little People must have had a hand in it, but Henry would never believe that. He touched her poor blue hands. They were clay cold. Her eyes opened and stared at him like two pale blue buttons. He knew then that she was just a human child, lost and far from home, cold and probably hunger-starved as well. Her mouth opened and she began to cry noisily. He had nothing much to warm her with, but with difficulty he managed to heave her up onto Jess's back. He sat up behind her, making his cloak wrap around both of them. He had to hold one arm around her all the time, as she could not balance herself at all, and she was stiff with cold. Jess seemed quite resigned to the extra burden and plodded on patiently through the mist.

The child's yowling soon turned to a steady whimper, and Henry hoped she would soon fall asleep so as to be less aware of her misery. She was in desperate need of hot drink and dry clothes and a warm bed, but it would be some hours yet before she could have them. She might be dead when he got her back to their farm, but there were likely no other farms near at hand, even if it were possible to see what there was more than a few yards round about. So nothing to do but go on.

Their road took them mostly up, though sometimes down, but at last it was certainly sloping more down than up, and Henry guessed that if the mist had lifted, Teesdale would have been in sight beneath them by that time.

The bairn was quiet at last, drooped back into unconsciousness again, but alive and getting warmer with the heat from Henry and Jess. Jess picked her way patiently downward but was beginning to tire. Henry prayed that she would not go lame, for if she did, they would never reach home that night and the little one would not last longer.

At last they were below the cloud, but the sunken sun had given place to a full moon. They were in sight of home, even nearer to it than he had durst hope or believe. But they were even nearer to the Collinson farm than to the Watsons, and Jess just about at the end of her strength. Henry thought that perhaps if they stopped there to leave Jess and give the Collinsons news of Hobby, they would give the bairn something to sup and a bit of warmth before he carried her on to his father's farm; that would be heavy work, though, but maybe he would be able to borrow a handcart or hay sledge to take her on.

They were only a few minutes' ride away from the Collinson farm when the bairn jerked awake and began wailing inconsolably all over again. Henry put his hand in his pouch despairingly, in the doubtful hope of finding some crumb of food or comfort there to quiet her. His hand touched the little stone "keepsake." It was a forlorn hope indeed, but he pulled out the small figure and held it close in front of her.

"There!" he said. "A little dolly for you!"

The effect was miraculous. The wailing stopped instantly, and though her mouth stayed open, it curved up into a smile that was like a new moon lying on its back. Her chilblained fingers, purple and swollen, tried to curl round the stone figure that was even colder than the hand that tried to grasp it. It fell straight to the ground and the wailing began again.

Henry jumped down with the child in his arms, took off his cloak, picked up the "dolly" and, wrapping dolly and child together tightly in the cloak, he slung the human parcel onto the horse's back. The child was peaceful enough then, but kept on repeating some word that he could not understand, over and over again, in a husky whisper.

At last they reached the Collinsons' door. By God's good grace she was still alive.

15

A New Home for Sarah

It was Hobby's grandmother that took the bairn from him, and gently rubbed her warm by the fireside, and gave her cow's milk to drink, and hapt her up in a big shawl, and gently rocked her to sleep in the old cradle that the other wheezy little lass had used to sleep in.

Hobby's mother had dropped onto the settle meanwhile, where she swayed to and fro, clasping and unclasping her hands and exclaiming about Hobby breaking her heart by going off to foreign places like that without so much as a word of farewell to his mother what had reared him; and didn't he know it were him, her own firstborn son Hobby, that she had been missing all these months? Not that lazy horse Jess!

But Hobby's father and the two up-grown daughters seemed pleased enough to have that lazy horse Jess back home again. The lasses were petting and stroking and feeding her, and asking plenty of questions in between about the battle and the soldiers, and what Henry knew of any of the lads from thereabouts who had hurried away to the war and not yet ridden home again. What could he tell them of William and Howard, Geoffrey and Richard and two or three Johns? For they were of the age when every other lad was a possible sweetheart, time was passing by, and any lad in uniform was reckoned someone special.

The Collinsons and the Watsons were the only Puritans living around there at one time; though soon it seemed that everyone was to be a Puritan, at least in his way of speaking and church going, whatever his thoughts might be. But Henry guessed it was some of the Royalists with their gayer uniforms that those lasses were hankering after, though they durstn't make it too plain with their parents there to hear every word that was said. But as all Henry's companions had been of Cromwell's army, it was little he could do to quench their curiosity.

Well, of course Henry was soon anxious to get away, out of the Collinson's kitchen and into his own. So he begged the loan of the lanthorn, and a cart if there were a spare one, to carry the child on home. The old grandmother would not hear of it.

"Leave her be for tonight!" she said. "She's deep asleep now, and she should stay asleep here in the warm. She'll be taken bad again if you disturb her now and take her out into the cold night air. You can come back in the morn and fetch her when she's had hersel' rested."

The bairn was certainly deep asleep, and looking real peaceful at last, hapt up in that shawl with the dolly tucked under her arm. There was common sense in what the old woman said, so, thanking them all, he took the lanthorn that Collinson had brought in for him and hurried out into the night.

What a welcome there was when he walked into the Watsons' kitchen a little while later! Father and mother were real glad to have him safely home, and the children were wild with excitement.

His young sister Marion was the oldest of the girls still left at home, not having started at the Turnbulls at that time, and she was talking like a burn in spate, the way she always did, telling everything that everyone had said and done since he had left Teesdale, asking questions and never pausing for an answer. His little brothers and sisters meanwhile were climbing all over him, poking their inquisitive fingers into pocket and pouch, searching for keepsakes or trifles brought back from Scotland likely, but they found nothing there. Even the small stone figure that he had thought to give his little sisters for a toy had been left behind at the Collinsons with that poor bairn. He was glad that they seemed to bear him no grudge for his forgetfulness.

It was not till the small ones had worn theirselves out and were all abed and sleeping and he had been given all the news of the neighborhood, that Henry told his mother about the little lass he had found lying unconscious on the fell there; and how he had planned to bring her home with him, but had been persuaded to leave her at the Collinsons till the morn, when he would ride over on their pony to fetch her.

"Poor lass!" his mother said. "It were a good chance you found her when you did, else she'd have died o' cold, likely, poor thing!"

"It was no chance," interrupted his father. "It was surely the good Lord led our Henry to her."

His mother nodded. "Aye," she agreed, "but what will we do with her when she's rested?"

"Do?" Henry asked. "I dunno that we'll have to do anything special with her, will we? She can stay here and play with Jenny and Margaret and Thomas, can't she?" He hadn't thought of anything beyond getting her safely home and warm and fed.

His mother fidgeted uneasily. "Well," she grudged, "it may be when she's grown up a bit she'll work toward her keep, but won't there be a family seeking her somewhere? Wanting her back, surely? Someone on this side or yon side o' the fell?"

It had never occurred to Henry that the bairn wouldn't be welcome to stay at the farm as long as always, maybe, and he felt a bit unsure about her working toward her keep, even when she had grown up a bit. He had said nothing to them about how he had thought once over that she could have been a duergar or some such; and he remembered how some had thought Collinsons' bairn wasn't mortal either and that she would never be any use or help in the house. He decided that perhaps he'd better keep such thoughts to himself till morning.

Then his father added his word.

True Puritan that he was, with a text ever ready on his

lips, he reminded them all of the Last Judgment, and how the Son of Man would come in his glory, telling the righteous that "I was an hungered and ye gave me meat; I was thirsty, and ye gave me drink; I was a stranger, and ye took me in; naked, and ye clothed me, I was sick and ye visited me . . ." and how the righteous had queried, and how they had been answered.

Henry and his mother waited to be sure he had finished right to the end, for Stephen Watson had such a rich flow of the Scriptures treasured in his head that it would not have done to interrupt before he reached the finish of it.

When he had ended the Bible words, Henry's mother was about to speak when her husband looked straight at her and said, "And the good Lord never said aught of the hungry, or the thirsty, or the sick or the naked strangers maybe helping toward their keep, neither! Even that Good Samaritan, who was only a poor human like the rest of us, never asked for payment for what he did. The lass should know where she belongs, and if she has a good Christian home, we must return her to it, certainly we must; but if not, she must make her home with us for as long as ever she needs it."

Mistress Watson bowed her head in agreement. She always took on Stephen's opinions, for he was a wise man, and able to read and write as well.

Henry was up and away before light next morning. He had said nothing to prepare his family for the kind of child he would be bringing back, for he could not think how best to say it.

Mistress Collinson was glad to see him and, he thought, to see the back of Sarah. They had decided that she must be called Sarah, Sarah Dooly, or Dolly, or Daly, or some name like that, for she repeated over and over again, "Sarah-dolly, Sarah-dolly, Sarah-dolly," and nothing else would she say, although they asked her plenty of questions, trying to find what her family was called and the place where she belonged. Only once did she say something different; after a long line of questions she smiled suddenly and said, "Not telling!" And that had made Mistress Collinson really vexed.

Sarah was still holding tight to the little stone figure in the old-fashioned clothes. She would not leave hold of it for an instant. They wrapped her in her own cloak that had been dried out by the fire and set her in front of Henry on the pony. She still could not balance herself properly, but at least she could sit up a little better than the listless lump that Jess had carried there the day before.

Henry thought they were relieved to wave them good-bye. All except the old grandmother. Sarah had filled a hole for her that had been left when the little crippled granddaughter had died the year before. Henry promised to bring Sarah back to see her as often as he could.

The Watson children, who had been waiting eagerly for the return of Henry and the little bairn, had come out onto the farm road to meet them, helloing and waving. Henry tried to persuade Sarah to wave back to them, but she was clutching her dolly with both hands and would not shift them. He took the pony into the yard and lifted Sarah down. Jenny and Margaret were jumping and skipping in circles around them, wild with joy at the prospect of a new playmate.

"Hello, little lass!" Jenny greeted her. "What do they call you?"

Sarah smiled her new moon smile, dribbled, and said nothing.

"Don't she talk?" asked Margaret, disappointed.

"Not much yet," Henry said. "She's still tired and poorly with lying out there in the cold on the fell. But we think she must be called Sarah."

He carried her inside and set her down on the little cracket in front of the kitchen fire. Everyone crowded around her.

"Look! She's got a funny little dolly!" cried Jenny, putting out her hand to touch the little stone figure. "A dolly with a big old-fashioned collar."

Sarah hugged the dolly closer to herself, guarding it jealously. Then she began rocking herself and it backward and forward and croaking an odd little lullaby. (When Henry told me that, I could but smile, remembering how she had once thrown a rag babby on the fire because she had wanted nothing but a little stone dolly for rock-a-bye! Now, it seemed, she had had her wish after all.)

Henry looked up at his mother, who was standing behind the children, leaning against the trestle table. She looked pale, and her voice stumbled.

"Henry," she said, "you never told me she were a shatter-pated bairn!"

Henry turned in desperation from her to his father. His father's face, as usual, was calm and grave. Then, smiling at Sarah, he nodded and said, "He took a child and set him in the midst of them; and when he had taken him in his arms, he said unto them, Whosoever shall receive one of such children in my name, receiveth me; and whosoever shall receive me, receiveth not me, but him that sent me."

Henry knew then that however shatter-pated Sarah might turn out to be, his father would have them give her a home. As long as he was there, Sarah would be all right. His father, and God, would somehow care for her between them.

16

Sarah Must Move On

*H*ow I wished that could have been the end of Henry's story! A happy ending with Sarah sitting there at the Watsons' fireside, rocking herself and her Sarah-dolly backward and forward to the tune of some croaky little song with words that no other mortal could understand; or playing with Margaret and Jenny and Thomas; getting in folk's way and doubtless being scolded for it, the way she used to be scolded at Wulsingham, but still smiling her happy, clowny smile; waiting for me there in Teesdale for the five years or so that were to pass before I met Marion Watson when we were both working at the Turnbulls, and, later, her brother Henry. Then they would have learned that "their Sarah" was my sister Sarah, Sarah Emerson from Wulsingham, for although Stephen Watson had tried to trace Sarah's parents, he had not managed to find them, so "our Sarah" stayed on at Cudderstane and became "his Sarah."

Whatever trouble that Hetty would have been set to

make then, I'm sure my good father and Henry's father would have come to some agreement together for Sarah to have a safe corner in their Cudderstane kitchen, or some other home out of Hetty's reach, for always. Maybe I'd have left the Turnbulls, good place though it was, and worked on a Teesdale farm instead, so I could keep an eye on Sarah. I would have liked that. I was already taken with the idea of being somewhere close to Henry.

Henry had said that as long as his father was there Sarah would be all right. It had never crossed his mind that before she had been with them a six-month his father would be dead. A big, healthy, clean-living man Stephen Watson had always been. He was struck down as suddenly as a tree in a lightning storm, and no one knowing even the name of the sickness that took him from them.

Everything changed at the Watson farm after that. There certainly were over-many lasses and not enough lads in that family then. All the heavy work of the farm and the managing of it fell to Henry. He had broad shoulders to take the load, with a good conscience and a warm heart to steer him, but he was only one where there had been two before; even though their little Thomas was a good, willing worker when he wasn't at school— for all he was not much above a yard high.

But Mistress Watson was a changed woman after her man was gone, like a one-legged cripple without a crutch. Good husband as he had been, it may be he had done too much for her, too much in the way of thinking and planning and deciding and knowing at every cross-road which was the right and Christian way to take.

Her being that distraught and uncertain-tempered, of course it was the smallest bairns, the ones who were under Mistress Watson's feet all day long, that suffered most from the flat of her hand and the sharp edge of her tongue. And none, you may be sure, as much as Sarah.

Henry certainly suspected something, though likely not all of the way things were going, for he was outdoors mostly, busy with the stock.

It was Marion who saw all the kitchen trouble, and the upset and the argue that Sarah made, and it was Marion who told me all about it.

"That Sarah!" she exclaimed. "The senseless mischiefs she would get up to! Picking up the peats from the hearth and dropping them into the maslin before it were baked! And if that were not enough, the next day she took our Henry's tall boots what were drying agin the fire and hurled them into the great caldron of water that was bubbling away there—how she had the strength to do it I can't say, but a miracle she didna scald hersel' and our Thomas to death that time, the sackless wench! She would've set the house afire, not once but many a time, if one o' us hadna grabbed her quick enough.

"And you know, Lucy," she rattled on, "it wasn't that we weren't patient with her, Mother and me. I spent long enough trying to teach that bairn the knitting, but she were never able to learn nowt. She dropped every loop I put on the needles for her, and was allus riving it up till it looked like a magpie's nest. And from time to time, and at all times, she would sit there grinning and slavering, grinning and slavering and rocking hersel' backward and forward."

Poor Marion! I thought. She was not the first to struggle to no avail with Sarah's knitting.

Naturally it was not long before Watsons' neighbors were whispering about Sarah in just the way our neighbors had whispered about her when she was living at home. Some of their whispers were pretty loud, more like a quiet shout.

"Not like an ordinary bairn, that one," they wagged. "She's bin tret too soft, likely, by them that had her afore Watsons did. Hannah Watson has plenty on her hands now without the likes of that one plaguing her! If they tret her the way she deserves to be tret with her silly, dirty ways, maybe They'd take her back. I've heard They take them back sometimes when they're harshly used. Changeling or no changeling, she's not the Watsons' bairn, so why should Hannah Watson be laden with her?"

Something of what they were saying no doubt came to Hannah's ears, the way that tatters of what is whispered behind the back often enough do drift around to the front; and no doubt it only favored what she herself was already thinking about Sarah.

So it was hardly surprising that as time went on Sarah was more and more roughly punished for the daft things she did, and, I don't doubt, for some of the daft things the other bairns did as well; for all bairns can act daft at times, even the cleverest ones, and the Watsons' bairns were no different from others that way.

In the end Mistress Watson was asking Henry quite openly and sharply to get rid of Sarah, an idea she would never have breathed aloud while Stephen Watson was living; nor would she have suggested then that Sarah wasn't human, but all the gossip about it, on top of what she had been wondering herself, made her sure there was something unearthly about the bairn, and as Henry had brought her in, it was for Henry to get rid of her, she said.

But it was not until Henry saw the great bruises on Sarah's arms and legs that he determined that, for her own sake, Sarah must go, and go soon. He guessed she could be roughly used by Marion as well as by his mother. It could be broken limbs or worse, next time. The difficulty was finding a home of any kind, but Henry was determined it should only be a good one.

He would have liked Hobby Collinson's granny to take her, but of late weeks the poor old lady had grown back into nothing but a silly little child herself, in no way fit to look after another. He doubted that living in the same house as Hobby's mother would be any better than living with his own mother, either.

At last, having racked his brains until his head was near to bursting, a sudden thought came to him. He made up his mind to take Sarah to his old aunt Emmeline—if only he could find her.

17

Henry's Aunt Emmeline

If Henry had not been such a plain, truthful man, I would never have believed what he told me about his aunt Emmeline.

Aunt Emmeline was Stephen Watson's older sister—much older. She had had her place in the Watson farmhouse ever since she had been born there, so that neither Henry nor even his father could remember a time when she was not busy about the place, or sitting there spinning or knitting of an evening; either way, singing when she had enough breath to sing with, or humming like a hive of bees when she hadn't.

She was a tiny spinster, lively and perky as a redbreast, with the kindest warm heart you could find anyplace. In bygone days there must have been much guessing as to why she never wed, for it did not seem possible that such a canny, good-natured, useful soul as she was had never been asked. She certainly had some odd little ways and eccentricities, as many old women do have, but nothing so strange as you could call mad or lunatic. Leastways, not until the night she upped and ran away, never to come back.

That would have been in the summer of 1648 by my reckoning, some two years before Henry joined Cromwell's army.

Henry's father and Aunt Emmeline had been all day at Barney Castle market. It was a fiercely hot day in July. Stephen had been selling some ewes, and Aunt Emmeline had her usual basket of eggs and Cudderstane cheese.

When it was time to go home, Aunt Emmeline was not waiting at the side of the cart for Stephen where she generally waited, nor was she at her usual selling place in the butter market.

After seeking her for some minutes, Stephen found her wandering among the crowds in Galgate in a sort of daze, her cheeks flushed and a happy smile on her mouth.

"Where've you bin, Emmeline?" he asked her.

She had seemed startled and confused when he spoke to her, and answered shortly, "I were talking with a shepherd."

All the way home she had sat very upright and silent, unlike her usual chattery self. Generally, after market, she was pouring out whom she had seen and what they were wearing, whom they were with, what they had said and what she had said back, so on and so on, all the way home.

She hardly spoke to anyone all that evening. It was

not until Henry and his father had gone up to bed, and Mistress Watson and she were alone in the kitchen and about to separate for the night, that she had drawn Mistress Watson to her, kissed her good night very lovingly and whispered, "It will be good night for a long time, Hannah. I am going away tonight with the man I love. May God bless you all!"

"Away?" cried Henry's mother. "Away to where? With a *man*? With what man?"

But Aunt Emmeline had only smiled and answered demurely, "Away with my shepherd man, to wherever he takes me."

Now, Mistress Watson had no doubt been startled by such a declaration, for it was hardly what one would look to hear from a spinster turned sixty, such as Henry's aunt Emmeline then was. Flighty young lasses might have their empty heads turned by romantic notions of running away with a lover, but not anyone as old as Aunt Emmeline, surely! And even flighty lasses would not have recklessly confided their secret before they left.

But Henry's mother knew that Aunt Emmeline had her peculiarities, talking to the buttercups or to the chairs and tables, or to herself if there was no one else to listen to her, and making daisy chains for the kittens, and she knew how old people's fancies tended to increase over the years. She had told them all later that she thought the sun that had been beating down so fiercely all day had perhaps turned the old lady's brain a little. So, after making a soothing posset, she left her alone down there in the kitchen without passing on a word to anyone of what had been confided to her.

I must say that if I had been in her shoes, I would have said something about Aunt Emmeline's strange proposal to someone else, and would myself have slept beside the old woman for fear she were taken worse in the night. But that is how it was. Mistress Watson didn't do any such thing.

Next morning, at sunrise, Aunt Emmeline was gone, without word or sound.

Such a commotion there must have been when it was discovered that she was missing! No one would have believed that she could have been up and away without waking man or beast.

Aunt Emmeline had always slept down there in the kitchen, the same as our old granny had done in our cottage. Not that she couldn't get up and down the loft ladder, for stairs and ladders were no trouble to her. Henry said she had the liveliest pair of legs in Cudderstane for the Morpeth Rant in the days before dancing and such were considered sinful. But she had always slept downstairs ever since she was a bairn and saw no reason to change, even if there had been room to spare above, which there wasn't.

The house door was unbarred, but there was no sign of cart tracks or hoof marks on the parched ground outside the house, and it seemed impossible that she could have left without setting the dog off barking or the geese gabbling. But gone she was, taking nothing but the clothes she had been wearing and her blue winter cloak.

"Witchcraft, it seemed like," Mistress Watson had said. "Plain mortals do not float away like thistledown in the middle of the night. She were allus different from others, that one! And it were no ordinary shepherd fetched her away, by my reckoning!"

Every corner of the house and byre was searched, and every chest and closet opened. Hidey-go-seek had always been a favorite game of Aunt Emmeline's, and some believed she might be playing it still, but not a trace of her could be found.

But though he could find no other explanation for his sister's complete disappearance, Stephen Watson frowned on any suggestion of magical happenings. Superstitious hocus-pocus was something he never would believe in.

18

The Search for Aunt Emmeline

For some months Stephen Watson searched the countryside looking for his sister Emmeline. Although he had been brought up as a strict Puritan and remained so all his life, he was well respected in that neighborhood, which had clung to the old religion more persistently than most. There were Watsons and Dents all through Teesdale like currants in a plum pudding, same as there are Pearts and Emersons all through Weredale. But these two Watsons, Stephen and Emmeline, were more than commonly well known and liked. Yet, though Stephen sought out and questioned all the farmers for miles around, there was not one who had seen anything of Emmeline since that market day at Barney Castle on the last Wednesday of July.

It wasn't long before all the well-known faces at Barney market had been asked, as well as some of the not so well-known ones. Travelers were questioned then, peddlers, faws and tinkers, different ones that were coming in from a distance each week, but it was hard to know what to ask of such strangers. It was easy enough for

Stephen to describe the bright-eyed little old lady, but whether to say she was with a young man or an old one, or alone, on horseback, in a cart or on foot, he did not know.

So it was little help that the peddlers and the faws and the tinkers were able to give, though they started up many a false trail. Some had recollections of having seen an old woman in this village or that town, who seemed something like the description of Emmeline Watson; an old woman sitting against a tree with an old man who might have been a shepherd; a small woman wearing a blue winter cloak on a day far too hot to be wearing a cloak at all; an oldish couple, both singing drunk, rattling down the road to Reeth in a rickety cart.

Stephen enquired of the parson in every parish within reach for the marriage of an elderly spinster or the crying of her banns, but none could give him any news such as he would have been glad to hear. He searched through those registers too, that they have to keep in churches nowadays, but there were no records in them of any Emmeline Watson being married. Perhaps they had gone as far as the border for a Scottish wedding. The more that was unexplained, the more guessing there was for the babble-mouthed gossips.

It must have been less than two years after his aunt Emmeline had eloped that Henry's father had a letter from a parson at Bowes in Yorkshire, delivered by the hand of a traveler, saying that he had that week buried a shepherd from the Stanemore Forest called Charles Watson, and might that be the shepherd that Stephen Watson was looking for? And if so, it might be of interest to him to know that his small, elderly widow was living lonely in a cottage on the Stanemore, by God's Bridge, he believed.

Well, if that were the case, Aunt Emmeline hadn't changed her name by marrying. That must have been the way with many a one in Teesdale with all those Watsons. Neither was being a shepherd any proof of being Aunt Emmeline's husband. There weren't much else but shepherds needed on land that was able to support little else but sheep.

But of course Stephen Watson and his son Henry wanted to ride over to God's Bridge straightaway, to see if it were really Sister or Aunt Emmeline living there. But as it was a fair ride and two could not be well spared from the farm, they decided that Henry should be the one to go.

He found the cottage, at length, though it seemed like a miracle when he did, for at first there had been no one to direct him, nor any building in sight after he left the bridge. Neither was the cottage as near to God's Bridge as the parson had made it sound, but much farther south into Yorkshire, toward Arkengarthdale. God's Bridge, if you do not know it, is a single great slab of limestone that stretches comfortably and conveniently across the little river Greta, from one half of Stanemore to the other. It was not put there by any human hand, so people say, but has always been there, ever since the creation of the world.

After at least two hours' more traveling that wild landscape beyond the bridge, skirting bogs and peat hags, he began to wonder whether he had lost his sense of direction and was wandering in aimless circles; so he was relieved to see a farmer carting peats that had been cut and stacked on the moor.

He enquired for a cottage where a Widow Watson was living.

The farmer shook his head. "No widow," he said. "Charlie Watson lives alone in his farm, about a mile over yonder, but he were never married," and he pointed the direction.

"Yes he were married!" said Henry. "Possibly to an Emmeline Watson, less than two year ago. He were buried last week."

The other man shrugged. "I never heard that," he said. "But I've bin no nearer the place than this for long enough. He could be married or dead for all I know; kept hissel' to hissel', like. Or maybe it were a different Charlie Watson?"

Henry agreed that it could be a different Charlie Watson, so he just thanked the farmer and made away in the direction that had been pointed.

Presently a little tumbled cottage, more than half down, came into sight. When he gained the threshold he could hear a frail, familiar voice singing the Hundredth Psalm.

Henry admitted that his aunt was welcoming, and seemed truly pleased to see him, as well as being in good health; but say what he could, there was no way he could persuade her to ride back to the farm at Cudderstane with him.

"This little house is my home," she said. "Here Charlie Watson and I have been happy together. We were not together long, but Charlie feels close to me here—not that I was not happy at Cudderstane for all those years, but I have my little garden with vegetables here, and here I will finish my days. Every evening a hedgehog comes and shares a cup of bread and milk with me, and what would the poor creature do if its supper were not set beside the door?" And half a dozen other silly excuses she made for not leaving the place. Stubborn as a mule she was about it!

On the way home from his fruitless journey Henry again saw the peat collector and bargained with him to take a supply of peats to the lonely farmhouse every month during the coming winter.

When Henry reached home alone, he was not able to convince his father that he had tried every possible trick to persuade Aunt Emmeline to come back with him. The thought of his sister alone in her old age and poverty in that crumbling ruin was a grave burden on Stephen's conscience.

So the next week it was Stephen himself who set out on the long ride beyond God's Bridge, to try to talk his sister into sharing their home with them again. But he, too, came home alone and silent, and Emmeline stayed where she was, singing, humming, and obstinately contented with her goat and her hens and her cat and her hedgehog.

It must have been just one year later, after Henry had been to the wars and come home again, bringing our Sarah with him, half dead on Hobby Collinson's horse, and his father, Stephen Watson, had died so suddenly, that Henry and Sarah and the little Sarah-dolly were once more riding south across rough, wild country.

This time Henry was taking them to his aunt Emmeline on the Stanemore.

19

Another New Home for Sarah

The cuckoo was shouting as Henry and Sarah and her beloved Sarah-dolly left Cudderstane that April morning.

"Cuck-oo!" answered Sarah happily, as usual. "Cuck-oo!"

There were larks singing, too, very high up, but Sarah wouldn't have heard them. It was, at any rate, a good start for the day, with Henry praying it would end as happily.

Mistress Watson had been thankful to see them go, and had taken trouble to provide plenty of provisions for their journey, with rye flour, oats, bacon and a few comforts for Aunt Emmeline, and a bundle of clothes for Sarah. She had no doubts that her sister-in-law would give Sarah a home—at least, as good a home as she deserved to have. The previous week Henry had overheard her chattering to her neighbor Mistress Collinson about it. "Two of a kind, that's what they are!" she had said. "They will be good company for one another."

And Mistress Collinson had nodded and said, "Aye.

There is something unnatural about the both of them, ain't there?"

The small Watson children were rather sad when they realized that Sarah was probably leaving them forever, for she had often joined in their games in a clumsy, good-natured sort of way, though at other times they did not want her; but I suspect that Marion was as pleased as her mother to see Sarah go.

The cuckoo and the larks were out of earshot long before they reached God's Bridge. It was the bubbling of the curlew that filled the air over Stanemore, a sound that was unfamiliar to Sarah, who tried to copy it without much success.

Henry and his father had each been back once to see Aunt Emmeline, soon after their first visit to Stanemore, and were satisfied that she was in good health and still full of song in her moorland home. But when Henry had marched away with Cromwell's army, his father had been too bound to the farm to go back there, and Henry felt rather put to the blush that he had been at home almost half a year before again making his journey across the Stanemore. Aunt Emmeline would know nothing of her brother's death, or of Sarah's existence.

Henry wondered how best to explain everything to his aunt, and began to have some small doubts about his impulse to leave Sarah with her as a companion, even though he would pay in money and in kind for her keep. The move would be a good one for Sarah certainly, and make everything much easier at the Watson farm, but what of the old lady? Was she perhaps too old to take the burden of looking after such a child as Sarah was? Fortunately she had always been fond of bairns, but Sarah was rather different from other bairns, and there were others beside his mother and Mistress Collinson who had found her a nuisance. It wasn't everyone had the patience to clear up all the messes she made, or could suffer her singing and shouting without irritation.

The pony needed little direction. As she picked her way through the ling, Henry began telling Sarah about Emmeline, about the songs she would sing, and the stories she might tell, and the good oatcakes she would make, and the cat and the goat and the hens and the hedgehog. But Sarah, as so often happened, did not seem to be listening. Henry realized then that she had dropped off to sleep.

Sarah was still asleep when they reached the end of their journey. The door stood open and from inside came the lively humming of that favorite Hundredth Psalm. Aunt Emmeline was still alive and well.

Henry lifted Sarah down and carried her, only half awake, into the kitchen. Aunt Emmeline stopped short in the middle of a verse and looked up. "This is a welcome surprise, Henry!" she said. "And whose little lass is that?"

Henry, to his own great astonishment, smiled and answered directly, "Yours, if you like to keep her, Aunt Emmeline."

"I should like that fine," the old woman said. "Good

company for me she'd be." So, after pondering and worrying all the morning as to the best way of putting his proposal before his aunt, the whole matter had settled itself in two shakes of a lamb's tail.

Sarah, meanwhile, had curled herself up on the floor and gone back to sleep with her arms around the cat. The cat, usually suspicious of strangers, was peacefully asleep as well.

"I did not think to outlive our Stephen" was Aunt Emmeline's only comment when Henry told her that his father was dead. She had been very fond of Stephen all her life, but she took his death as casually as she had seemed to have taken Charles Watson's death. She never spoke more of Charles Watson. None of us ever found out what sort of man he had been, only that Aunt Emmeline had loved him and he had made her happy.

She listened quietly to Henry's story of finding Sarah on Bollyop Fell. She even stopped knitting for a few minutes of the telling of it.

Then, hesitating, and choosing his words carefully, Henry tried to explain the difficulty of having Sarah in that busy household at Cudderstane, for he would not speak ill of his mother, nor did he want to blame Sarah for all the fratch there was at home at that time.

Emmeline Watson did not need his explanation. Before he had barely started on it she said, "Your mother were always hasty with bairns, especially little uns. That bairn will be better here with me, so long as ever she cares to stay, or I am here to look after her."

So that was that.

Henry gave her the bacon and the oats and the rye, and Sarah's clothes and some money with them, and a promise to bring more next quarter day.

Aunt Emmeline would have taken Sarah willingly enough, even if they had come empty-handed. As it was, she just smiled gently and said, "Thank you. With the eggs, and goat's milk, and my vegetables, I think I eat as well as most, with enough to share with the little lass an' all. Though I'd certainly be well pleased to see you, or Marion or any of the other children, any time they were able and had a mind to ride over such a distance."

Henry noticed that she did not include his mother in her invitation. He begged her to let him know if there was anything she would like him to bring from the market next time he came, for there was nowhere near at hand for her to buy anything at all.

But she only smiled and said, "Thank you. We have everything we need."

With Sarah so happily asleep down there with the cat and her Sarah-dolly, Henry deemed it best not to wake her to say good-bye, so, taking an affectionate leave of his old aunt, he rode back to Cudderstane.

Henry went back to the Stanemore regularly after that, on quarter days, taking grain and flour for the two of them, and sometimes a moorcock or partridge from the fell, which Aunt Emmeline accepted happily, though she never asked for anything. There were small toys, too, that he and his little brother Thomas had made together for Sarah. Sarah was always dribbling, smiling, and happy as ever.

As time went on the two seemed to be slowly changing places. As Sarah grew bigger, little Aunt Emmeline seemed to be shrinking as she became frailer, though still lively and full of song. Sarah played with the old lady as another child might have played with a big doll; clumsily buttoning and unbuttoning her clothes, tucking the shawl more closely around her, and, of course, singing husky little lullabies when she thought it was time for Aunt Emmeline to go to sleep.

Each time he visited them Henry was satisfied that all was well with that oddly assorted household in the lonely cottage out there on the Stanemore.

20

Witch Talk

*A*t the Barney Castle market, the last week of
September in 1652, Henry heard the young fel-
lows in that alehouse down near the Tees bridge
talking about some witch woman who was living on
Stanemore; a witch was what they were calling her,
though an older man insisted, "She's no witch till she is
proved a witch. She's not bin proven, not tested by
pricking, nor by swimming, nor by any way as yet."

"She's a witch and no mistaking!" a burly man
answered. "There's bin plenty trouble just beyond hereabouts, lately. Cattle have bin sickening all over
between here and Appleby—an' not cattle only, neither.
Three children at different farms at Bowes were taken
with fits in the same week, and two of John Dent's horses
died in one week for no natural reason. They were
overlooked, for certain. And there's a Richard Ward
that farms by Bowes and cuts peats on the Stanemore,
says she has two familiars living with her; a cat and a
hedgehog."

Henry became very uneasy when he heard that about

the hedgehog. It was not as though there were plenty other people living on Stanemore, and even if there were, surely not with a hedgehog!

He usually kept apart from any such talk of witchcraft. Strict Dissenter though he was, he believed the Puritans were often over-ready to condemn their neighbors as witches, and that idle gossip on the subject only added to the false suspicions. But he could not contain his curiosity and anxiety for long, and felt bound to ask the name of the woman they were accusing.

"Wilson," said the burly drinker. "Wilson they call her—or is it Watson?"

"Aye, Watson it is," answered another. "But not Stanemore bred. Come from somewhere else."

"If she's bin makin' trouble," added another, "they should swim her afore she makes more. There's plenty watter in the Greta."

Henry did not wait to hear more. He had done most of his market business and what was not done, he left undone, and drove himself back to Cudderstane at full gallop.

It was wanting a few days to quarter day, when he would be going to Stanemore again to see Sarah, but he decided that those few days might well find him too late.

Saying nothing to his mother of the talk he had heard, he made arrangements to leave the farm at dawn next day.

It was high noon as Henry approached the crumbling

farm cottage on the moor. A hot, sultry day for autumn, but the door, so often standing open, was shut. As Henry alighted from his pony, he noticed the little stone Sarah-dolly lying on the midden. It seemed a strange place for Sarah to have put it, for it was seldom out of her hand.

Henry knocked at the door. There was no response from inside.

He knocked again, louder.

At his third knocking he heard a shuffling inside, and then the sound of bolts being drawn back. He could not remember that his aunt had ever bolted the door, certainly not in daylight.

The door creaked open a hand's breadth, and a leathery, twitching face appeared. It was nothing like Aunt Emmeline's.

"Watcher want?" bleated the old face.

"I have come to see my aunt, Emmeline Watson," said Henry.

"Not here!" said the crone, shutting the door.

Henry tried to put a foot over the threshold, but was too late; the bolts were already creaking back into place.

"Open again! If you please!" he shouted, but the door stayed shut. He could hear wheezy breathing on the other side of it. She was still very close to him.

"Can you tell me where Emmeline Watson has gone?" Henry called. "And the child, Sarah?"

"Never seen or heard of any such," came the wheezing answer. "This is my house now, so get you away back to where you came from!"

Henry made a last desperate appeal to her to give him some news of Aunt Emmeline. "Widow Watson lived here before you did, and her husband Charles Watson before her. Charles Watson died two year ago. Do you know where she and the child have gone? When did they leave this house? How long have you lived here?"

There was a long silence. At last, from farther inside the house came the threat, "Get you away from here! Them that meddles with my business may live to rue it!"

It was no use talking more, and quite plain to Henry that he would get no help from the old gammer. Turning aside, he picked up the old Sarah-dolly and dropped it into his pouch. Then he mounted his pony and moved off in the direction of Bowes, hoping that the parson or someone there would be able to give him news of Sarah and Aunt Emmeline.

But his hopes soon faded when he reached the village. There had been a few old women buried during the summer, but all well known to the parson, and none had been living on Stanemore or resembled Henry's description of Aunt Emmeline in any way. There were no Watsons in the burial register of recent date.

The parson answered all Henry's questions as briefly as possible, as though the talk were making him feel uncomfortable.

Henry tried to find out if anything was known of the woman who was living in the cottage that had once belonged to his aunt. Did the parson know her name?

Was it perhaps Wilson? Or even, perhaps, another Watson?

The only answer that came was a shake of the head and a shrug of the parson's shoulders.

Then there was a mumbled admission.

"I never saw that farmer, or shepherd Watson, above twice or thrice before I buried him. He was never at any church services in this parish since I came to Bowes six years ago. Nonattendance at church is, as you know, a punishable offense; he could have been fined up to twenty pounds a month for it, but I suppose it is too late now. Neither was he married in Bowes church, and I have heard nothing of the ceremony being performed in any other parish either. I never saw his wife—the woman you say was your aunt. She never came to church, no more than he did."

Henry said, "It is a long way for an old lady to walk from that cottage to Bowes church, even as lively an old body as my aunt Emmeline. And the little lass," he went on, in spite of the parson's disapproving expression. "Have you heard aught of a bairn that was living in that old cottage with her?"

The parson seemed surprised. "A bairn?" he cried. "Your father said your aunt was past sixty when she was taken away by Charles Watson. She would have had no lawful bairn from him; nor bairn nor grandbairn from any other, if, as he said, she had been a spinster all her life till then."

Henry told then how Sarah had been found so near to death on Bollyop, and how he had later taken her to his aunt for safekeeping, so as she would have a kindly foster mother.

The parson stayed silent for a long time, then he blurted out, "Tell me about this child! Was she a natural kind of girl? Just like an ordinary mortal girl, was she?"

Henry guessed what he was thinking, and dreaded hearing his fears put into words.

"Sarah was a cheerful and affectionate bairn, as I knew her," he said cautiously and truly.

"I never knew there was a child living in that place with Widow Watson," said the parson. "I have never set eyes on that ruined cottage myself. But I have heard some strange tales of late about a small creature that has been seen near Mirk Fell Gill on the far edge of Stanemore Forest, wandering alone, singing and laughing to itself in an unearthly manner. Shepherds have been disturbed by it, and none durst approach it to see what it was, for they believe that the Little People hate to be spied on. They tell of unaccountable happenings, too, and talk of witchcraft on the moor. No one has as yet asked me for exorcism, but if they do, I could not shirk my duty. Nor would the constable and I hesitate to bring to justice any who deal in evil spirits. For you must know that in the Book of Exodus it is written, 'Thou shalt not suffer a witch to live.'"

Henry nodded. He had heard it only too often. But he had never thought of it as something that might threaten anyone in his own family. He knew that unless he could find Aunt Emmeline soon, her life could be in terrible danger.

He remembered how, at the end of March in 1650, twelve women had been hanged for witchcraft in Newcastle because they did not bleed when pricked with needles by a Scottish witch-finder; a rogue of a conjurer he was, claiming twenty shillings for every conviction from his faked needles, and escaping away across the Scottish border himself, where he was never brought to justice.

Henry would not wish that fate on any woman; not on the churlish beldame who was living in Aunt Emmeline's tumbledown farmhouse, but most certainly not on Aunt Emmeline herself. He must save her at any price.

So Henry thanked the parson for what he had told him, disturbing though it was, and set out again for home, determined not to rest till he had some news of the old woman and the little girl, if he had to seek them in every parish of Yorkshire and beyond.

21

The Search in Swaledale

It was not till Henry had enquired in several other parishes near to Bowes that he rode, one fine September morning, much farther south, down into Swaledale.

He had talked the day before with a saddler in Barney Castle, whose brother had told him of a poor old soul who had lost her wits and been found wandering in Muker, down in Swaledale. This brother's wife had taken the harmless wanderer into their house to give her a bite and sup, for she looked half starved, when the poor body collapsed there in the kitchen and died with no one knowing who she was or where she came from.

The saddler supposed she had been buried by the parish in Muker, but he knew nothing more of her story.

Muker was a very long step on yon side of Stanemore, much farther than Bowes on this side, and the chance of the old vagabond being his aunt Emmeline and having walked so far was a small one. Though with Emmeline Watson the improbable often turned out to be more likely than the probable, and she did have those remarkably lively legs.

So, as nothing had been heard of her on the north side, Henry decided that, as a last bid, he had no hope but to try the unfamiliar dale to the south.

Taking directions from the Barney saddler for finding his brother, one James Thompson, Henry set out across the rough, high land over Stanemore and Tan Hill down into Swaledale.

The Thompsons' tiny house in the heart of Muker village was not hard to find. Henry was relieved when its door opened promptly to his knock, and that the rosy wife who stood there gave him such a warm welcome as soon as she heard that he had come from her brother-in-law at Barney Castle. She was full of sympathy when he told her of the disappearance of his eccentric old aunt, and his fear that it might even have been she who had found her way to Muker, only to end her life there.

"A very small owd woman, desperate thin" was Mistress Thompson's description of the stranger she had brought into her kitchen to die, some ten weeks earlier. "But no name could we learn from her, nor where she came from neither, for she would say nowt when she were indoors, and paid no heed to our questioning. Dazed and puzzled she were, looking around, in front an' behind, everywhere, as though she were searching for summat; same as she were searching in the street where she were running from this side to that, calling, 'Where are you, luv? Where are you?' when James found her there on yon side o' t' church."

"Was she looking for someone called Sarah?" Henry had asked. "There was a bairn called Sarah living along with her, they were real fond of one another, and if it were my aunt you found and took in so kindly, it was doubtless Sarah she'd be looking for."

Mistress Thompson could not say. Her husband James would have likely mentioned it if he had heard any name, but he would be back from the byre soon, and would tell all he knew.

"What was she dressed in?" Henry asked.

"She were wearing this," said Mistress Thompson, opening the door of a big press and taking out a blue mantle, faded and worn, but with a very familiar look to it. Henry had little doubt then that it was his aunt Emmeline's mantle that she was showing him.

"They buried her here?" he asked.

"Aye," replied Mistress Thompson. "In t' churchyard there. I can show you her grave."

Henry followed her the few yards to the peaceful patch of consecrated ground that surrounded the little thatched church. There were but few stones in it, and a fresh grave stood out clearly, with a rosebush newly planted above it.

Aunt Emmeline had been no younger than most who died, and this was as good a place for her to lie in as another, when it was her time to lie. Her soul was certainly in Paradise now, and the rosebush, surely planted by the Thompsons, was proof that her earthly remains did not rest among unfeeling strangers. How thankful he was that she had not been buried at a crossroads with a stake driven through her heart, the fate of so many poor old eccentrics who fell into the hands of overzealous, superstitious witch-hunters of that time.

When they returned to the Thompsons' house, James Thompson was back from the byre. He could tell Henry no more than his wife had told already. He had not heard the old woman call the name Sarah but she had most certainly been searching for someone.

Perhaps she has found her, and they are together again now, Henry thought to himself. For what chance had any bairn to survive alone in that windswept waste of bog and stones?

Henry asked if they had heard of any stranger child being found in the neighborhood, but they both shook their heads.

Promising to return when he could, and let them know if he heard any news of Sarah, he went to see the vicar of Muker church.

The vicar, a kindly man, listened with great interest and sympathy to the story of Widow Watson and Sarah. He had been saddened by the plight of the old woman he had buried a few weeks before, and together they looked in the register where it was written, "Female unknown. Buried 31 July 1652." There was little doubt that that was Aunt Emmeline, and he promised that the "female unknown" would be changed to Emmeline Watson.

He was sorry he could tell Henry nothing about Sarah. "If a child had been found in Swaledale, I would have heard about it sooner or later," he assured him. "Mine is a large parish, and everything that happens in Keld or Grinton comes to my ears. I know little of what goes on beyond the dale to the north, where you say Widow Watson came from; it is a wild country, and there are tales of ghostly happenings up above the fells there, and over the tops. Ignorant folk talk of spirits and Little Folk haunting a place called Mirk Fell Gill, but I do not listen to old wives' trattles of ghosts and boggarts and Little People."

Henry did not usually listen to old wives' trattles either—but he still needed to find Sarah. This was the second time in a week that he had heard of supernatural creatures by Mirk Fell Gill. Certainly he did not think that Sarah had been stolen by fairies there, but he himself had once wondered if she was a duergar, hadn't he? Could it be that others, seeing or hearing her from afar, had thought as he had thought?

He decided that he must return by Mirk Fell Gill to search for any trace he could find of Sarah, long way around though it was. If she was wandering alone in that wild place she surely could not stay alive for long. There was no time to lose.

It was a rough pull over Stonesdale for the faithful pony; and Mirk Fell Gill was as bleak a place as it sounded. They crossed the turbulent gill, and scrambled up the highest point in sight. There was no sign of other human life from up there, or, indeed, of any other life at all. Partridge, pheasant, curlew and hare seemed to have deserted it. Henry dismounted and stood listening to the sound of his own breathing, for there was nothing else to hear. No insects hummed or droned in the ling at his feet, and the air was as still and quiet as in a painted landscape.

The sun was sinking, and the late September air turned chill. Henry was glad that Mistress Thompson had insisted on returning his aunt Emmeline's winter cloak to him; it would, at least, be a little extra warmth to wrap around Sarah when, and if, he found her.

Leading the pony, he crossed and recrossed the desolate waste, looking down every ravine and behind every boulder, stirring the clumps of bracken with a stick, calling, "Sarah! Sarah!" as he went.

There was no answering call.

Henry had no choice, after two hours' fruitless search, but to mount again and hurry back to Cudderstane through the dark, admitting he was beaten.

22

The Return to Wulsingham

For months after that Henry would still stop to question anyone he saw who had come from a distance—peddlers, traveling preachers and market traders—for any news of the finding of a wandering child. There never was any such news, though.

A few of them that had known Sarah felt sure that her own parents had somehow traced the child at last and taken her back home, though others simply said that she had been "taken back"—meaning by the Little Folk. But most, like Henry himself, reckoned that she must have wandered away and perished in some lonely place where she never would be found.

It was four years after Henry had found his aunt Emmeline's grave in the churchyard at Muker in Swaledale that I first met him when he came over to the Turnbulls to see Marion on her birthday, like I said, and he told me all that I have been telling you in these last chapters. Of course, I told him then all there was to tell of the first five years of Sarah's life and how suddenly she had disappeared from Wulsingham, with no one knowing whether she was stolen or just wandered off and not able to find her way home, and not a whisper of what had happened to her in all that time since. Henry had no doubt then, any more than I had, that it was our Sarah he had found up there, cold on the fell, taking, maybe, two days or more to reach the high place where he first came across her.

At the end of the next year Henry and I were married, and I went to live at the Watson farm in Teesdale.

Henry showed me the battered little Sarah-dolly that he had hoped one day to be able to return to Sarah. It seemed so strange to see it there in his hand. I thought how pleased Sarah must have been when Henry gave it to her that time when she was so cold and frightened and hungry up there on Bollyop, and I told him how we had both loved a whole family of little alabaster dollies when we were children. We put the dolly in the little wooden chest that Henry had made for me, to wait in there for Sarah; we would not allow anyone but Sarah to play with it.

Although our common sense should have told both of us that Sarah must surely be dead and playing happily in Paradise by this time, I don't think Henry really stopped looking for that bairn until the day he died—just keeping his eyes and ears open for her, hoping against hope.

I had not been married from my father's house. Of course I wanted to show Henry to my father, and show my father to Henry, for I was proud of them both. But it would be difficult for us to leave the farm at Cudderstane so as to make the journey over to Wulsingham. Everyone and everything at the Cudderstane farm depended so much on Henry, and I knew it would be an uneasy meeting for all of us at Wulsingham with Hetty always there. So I kept putting off the visit, hoping for a time that would somehow be easier—next month, perhaps, or next summer, but never today.

But I waited too long. My father never did see Henry, who died, just as his own father had died, far too young.

Henry himself would, I know, have simply said it was God's will that he died when he did. But I did not think so. I thought there was more of the Devil's will than God's in taking such a good man from me afore he was thirty year old, and afore we had been blessed with any bairns of our own.

So there I was, "Sister Lucy" in that busy, noisy farmhouse at Cudderstane, feeling as lonely sometimes as I would alone in a hermit's cell. I was fond enough of Thomas and Margaret and Jenny, but I could never love them the way I used to love our Sarah and Henry, and the way they all loved each other in spite of their childish fisticuffs and bickerings. Henry's mother and I were never very happy together, some way.

After I had been a widow for three years, and those Watson children were no longer bairns, excepting, perhaps, wee Jenny, Marion Watson came over on Mothering Sunday to see Mistress Watson, bringing news for me at the same time.

It seems that my sister Martha had told her that Hetty was no longer living with our father at Wulsingham. She had up and vanished away with a Scottish packman she had met at Stanhope Fair weeks before, and had never been seen or heard of since. My father, who was middling elderly by then, had been ailing for some time, Martha said.

It didn't take me long to decide that if my father was old and lonely and poorly over here in Weredale, and I was young and lonely and healthy over there in Teesdale, we might both do better living alongside one another.

The thought began to grow into a strange homesickness for our old home in Wulsingham marketplace, and the company of my quiet, gentle father.

So it wasn't long before I borrowed the farm pony for a day and rode over to Wulsingham with young Thomas, who insisted on accompanying me as an escort across the wild moors of Bollyop and down into Weredale.

Martha was in the old house when we arrived, and real glad they both were to see me. Martha had been coming through from Frosterley more days than she could rightly spare, to do what she could for our father, but with four little bairns of her own to see after, there was not that much time for nursing a sick man four mile away. His good neighbor Mistress Charlton did what she could, but she had too many years and ailments herself by this time to be much help, and our kind uncle William was dead.

There was no sign of the new Sarah. She would have been fourteen year old by that time, and could have been useful with it. When I asked after her, Martha told me she had started in place at a farm near Tow Law just before Hetty left, but if I hadn't come back when I did they'd have had to fetch her back from there to look after her father, just as she was settled and doing nicely.

So Thomas and the pony returned to Cudderstane without me. Thomas promised that if I did not return to the Watson farm within the month he would pile such bits of furniture as could truly be called my own onto the cart and drive them over to Wulsingham for me. Kind-hearted he was. Most of the furniture of the farm rightly belonged to my mother-in-law Mistress Watson, but there were a few little pieces that Henry had fettled himself—he was good with his hands—and I treasure the two crackets and the small rocking chair and the little chest he had made for me, the one where we kept the old Sarah-dolly, stubbornly waiting for Sarah.

My father had heard something of Henry's finding, and later losing, Sarah, from Martha by way of Marion, and, of course, he had heard of my marriage to Henry in the same way. It was plain to me that if he could have had his own way, he would have been at our wedding seven years before, as we had wanted him to be. But as long as that Hetty was in the house, he did not have his own way; a terrible harsh jailer she must have been.

My father was never one to speak ill of anyone, and his chest was that bad he was hard put to it to say anything at all, good or ill, for the coughing it would bring on when he tried to speak, but he did say to me, "That Hetty Bell was the biggest mistake I ever made, Lucy. Pray to God for me that she never returns."

And that was the longest talk I had from him that day, though it was twelve year since we had seen each other.

When I saw the poor state my father was in, and how glad he was to have me with him, I knew I must stay where I was for as long as he needed me; and I knew, too, that I would need no persuading to stay even beyond that time.

It was after I had been home for about a week that the door opened one afternoon and a big man walked into the kitchen whom I didn't recognize at once as my brother Richard.

Like me, Richard had left home almost as soon as Father had married Hetty Bell and no doubt for the same reason. He had gone as a hind to a Stanhope farmer. Martha had already told me how he had married the farmer's daughter Isabella, and they were living with her parents at Stanhope and he wasn't over-happy with the arrangement.

"Hello, Lucy!" he said. "I thought you were in Teesdale forever! It's long years since you came to see your poor old father."

I could but agree, though I excused myself by saying, "I'd have been over soon enough if I thought he was poorly and on his own, but he had Hetty Bell looking after him, didn't he?" From what our Martha had told me I don't think Richard had been there so often himself, though the journey from Stanhope was a deal easier than from Cudderstane. But I held my peace on that score, for I knew none of us had felt welcome there after there was a new mistress in the house. Even the new Sarah, who had never known any different, was glad to get away from the place the minute she had turned fourteen year old.

Richard laughed at the idea of Hetty looking after anyone except herself. He said no more on the subject, but went up the loft ladder to find his father wheezing pitifully on the big bed.

When he came down again he was full of talk about Isabella's parents—what was wrong with them and their house, and how Isabella and their two boys disliked living there; and how this house at Wulsingham would be a much better one for a growing family to thrive in; and how he could use our father's bit of land to good advantage, and turn the few goats and the scratch of hens into a proper farm.

Of course we all looked for the old house to go to Richard in my father's will, him and Martha being the eldest, and him the only lad. But for all that, I didn't think it right the way he was talking as though it were his already, and especially the way he said that when he and Isabella had the house perhaps they might let me stay on, sleeping downstairs on the settle, the way our old granny had slept when we were bairns. I didn't like the way he sounded as though they'd be doing me a great favor, nor did I fancy myself as an old fireside granny, being but six and twenty at the time, though I guessed the settle was as comfortable a place to sleep on as any—especially wintertime.

I feared at the time that my father was not long for this world, but I was wrong. With the spring there came a slow improvement in his health, and we lived happily together there for several years after that.

No more was ever heard of Hetty in those parts, and good riddance to her, I say. She had, after all, driven all us Emersons away from our own home at one time or another.

Meanwhile Richard had his own farm, for Isabella's parents had both died before Father did, and, their not having any lads, the farm had gone to Isabella's husband, so he was satisfied, though he did grumble about the house not being as big as he needed for all the children Isabella kept presenting him with. He could make no better of it, though, because to everyone's surprise the Wulsingham house was willed to me when my father did die, seeing as all the others had farms or homes of their own and were doing well (even the new Sarah had become Sarah Peart by marrying her sweetheart, young Sam Peart). That made me the only one left without a place of my own to live in, is what he said, so he set that right for me.

So I have this old house now for the rest of my life, and there is certainly no place would suit me better to end my days in than this, where I started from.

23

Alice – or Sarah?

*W*ith me having that house all to myself, that solid stone building that had once sheltered our family of seven comfortably enough, and having been a widow for a few years (though not yet halfway through the threescore years and ten that the psalmist leads us to hope for), it was hardly surprising that a few of the bachelors and widowers should make offers of marriage to me.

Apart from all I could do in the way of spinning and baking and cleaning and minding the chickens and all the things that every woman has to do, a home like that could be a great attraction, along with the money my father had left me, for I had been well provided for. How he came to have so much to share among us all I never did understand, nor how he kept Hetty Bell's grasping fingers off it, neither. He must have kept it well hid at one time, though after she was gone it lay where any of us could see it, for he trusted all of us, the way we all trusted him.

But I had no wish to marry any of those who made the

suggestion to me, for none could have held a candle to my Henry, and I was not willing to settle for second best.

So I have lived alone now in our old house from the day my father died until this. A lonely life it's been, though, and it's often and often I've wished I had Henry and our Sarah to share my hearthside, and wondered what they would look like now if they had lived, Henry at sixty-seven and Sarah at fifty-five year old. That is how old they'd have been when last year ended and we started on the new century, the year 1700, with all the strife between Cavaliers and Roundheads forty year behind us, and kings and queens on the English throne again ever since.

There were days when I felt that Sarah was a little ghost, hiding somewhere in this cottage where she had hidden herself so often when she was a bairn. There were times when I have come in from the garden and have thought I heard her thick, heavy breathing coming from underneath the settle, or behind the cloaks that hang from the wooden pegs beside the door. Often at night I have wakened suddenly and thought it was loud snoring that had roused me, but when I listened again there was only silence. Once when the cat was chasing a daddy-long-legs I'm sure someone laughed, and it wasn't me, and no other mortal in the house at the time, of that I am certain.

It was cuckoo time in this same year, 1700, that my sister, Sarah Peart, came to see me. She came through from time to time when her husband, Sam, had dealings in Wulsingham on market day, but it was a long time since she had last been.

I had seen all her grandbairns in turn, shortly after they were born, all except the last one, for Sarah Peart was a real proud grandmother. You'd think each one of them was her own firstborn bairn, the way she used to show them, and the way she used to spoil them all too. What a difference from our old granny, who never had a good word to say for any of us!

Yet my sister had never had much to say about Alice, her lastborn grandchild, the way she had about all the others. No boasting of how soon she was walking or talking or cutting her teeth. I doubt she ever told us anything Alice had ever done beyond getting herself born and christened.

I had never set eyes on the bairn before, so when she walked in with her grandmother that morning I was so startled I had to sit down quickly, my legs were melting away that fast. Alice looked as like to our lost Sarah as one rook looks to another. The same rather flat face, the spiky hair, the blue buttony eyes, the friendly, clowny smile, and the thread of dribble on her chin.

It was just as though our Sarah had walked straight back from wherever she had walked away to, all those fifty years ago.

"May I leave the bairn with you for a while, Lucy?" my sister Sarah asked. "Her mother is feeling right poorly with another on the way, and this one here is a fine one for poking her fingers into everything, and not giving a body a minute o' peace and quiet. I said we'd take her to the market to give Jane a bit o' rest like, but Sam's needing help with the selling, and this one'd be up to no end o' mischief—losing hersel' among them stalls, and wandering off with the tinkers and peddlers as like as not. She will stop with anyone, and make you no trouble, I'm sure."

Then she turned to Alice, threatening, "And I'll bray you when I get back if you misbehave for your great-aunt Lucy, mind!"

"Alice stay with Lucy." Alice smiled up at me, friendly, as though she had known me all her life.

"With *Great-aunt* Lucy," Sarah Peart corrected Alice sharply.

"Leave her with me," I said. "Leave her with me as long as ever you like."

Her grandmother muttered something under her breath that sounded rather like "You can keep her forever for all I care!" but I didn't think it would have really been that, would it? If that were really what she meant, I think I would have been willing to take her at her word there and then, Alice seeming so like to my first sister Sarah.

Alice seated herself on Henry's little cracket at the fireside while her grandmother was talking and rocked herself backward and forward, backward and forward.

She was quite at home in my kitchen and did not seem to notice when Sarah Peart went out, leaving us alone together.

After a time she began singing—no words, no tune, just the same sort of "singing" I had heard all those years before, so that I began to clap my hands slowly as I used to do for Sarah's singing, and Alice laughed and joined in the clapping.

I was needing more water, so we went out to the well for a bucketful. There were scraps to be given to the chickens, too, while we were out there. The sun was hot in the garden, and the birds were shouting.

"Cuck-oo! Cuck-oo!" Alice joined in.

A redbreast in front of the hedge cocked its head and winked at us.

The daisies were growing thick in the grass near the wall, and Alice snatched a handful of their heads. I showed her the right way to pick, with long stalks, but I doubt if she understood. We sat down on the doorstep and I made a daisy chain for her. She laughed when I put it around her neck. I hoped she would leave it on.

We stayed out there in the sun awhile, talking to the daisies and chickens till it had turned noon. Then we went inside and drank some broth from the big caldron that is always standing on the hearthside.

When Alice had finished slurping her little pipkinful of broth, she looked around the kitchen inquisitively, and I minded what her grandmother had said about her being a fine one for poking her fingers into everything and not giving a body a minute's peace. So I thought it best to find something to occupy her.

I could have brought the Sarah-dolly out of its hiding place for Alice to play with, but it had been waiting for our Sarah for so many years that I didn't want to take it out till I was sure—not till I was absolutely sure.

So, instead, I dressed a wooden spoon in a kerchief for Sar— I mean Alice, and she rocked happily with it in her lap while I drowsed and rocked in the rocking chair beside her. I was put in mind of how angry our Sarah had been with her rag babby, and I fell to wondering, as I had wondered many a time before, whether Sarah was really in Heaven as Henry used to say she was. If she were dead, which we thought she must be, someone would surely have found her and she'd have been buried by the parish like Aunt Emmeline, if they didn't know who she was and no one claimed her. Supposing she had been found by them that thought she didn't look like a proper natural bairn, she'd still have been buried in the churchyard, even if it were only on the north side. But Henry had searched the graveyards near and far, all sides of them, for small new graves, and found nothing. It was always the north side for those that would find the gates of Paradise shut fast against them: murderers, suicides, witches sometimes, and any that had dealings with evil spirits and suchlike—and maybe changelings?

Changelings, fairies, Little People, boggarts and duergars. We don't hear so much of them-such nowadays. The Puritans taught that the only spirits were God and

His Angels and the Devil. They had plenty to say about the Devil, but all the others excepting God and His Angels, they said, were evil, pagan superstitions. So there are plenty boasting nowadays that they cannot believe in such hocus-pocus, and they have what they call a scientific reason for explaining any strange happenings that occur, instead of blaming the fairies, duergars or witches even. Though much that some call scientific I would say was just plain common sense.

I had never believed that Sarah was a changeling, but I must have believed in changelings, or how could I believe that she wasn't one?

So if there were changelings, there must have been fairies, and mightn't they have stolen Sarah away anytime she wasn't wearing a daisy chain, even after she was living on the Stanemore? And if, after many years, she had escaped her captors, wouldn't it be only us who had grown older, and not her?

At last I could keep all my confused thoughts to myself no longer.

"Sarah," I said, "tell Lucy where you have been all this long time."

Alice looked up at me at once. Seemingly, it made no difference to her that I had accidentally called her Sarah.

"Not telling!" was all she said.

Glossary

argue	argument
babby	baby
bairn	child
beldame	old woman
bit sup	little drink
boggart	specter or phantom
bray	beat
bumler	bumblebee
burn	brook
byre	cow shed
cracket	low wooden stool
duergar	bad-tempered dwarf (supernatural)
durst	dared
faws	gypsies
fell	high moorland
fettle	put in good order or make by hand
fireback	back of fireplace
fratch	quarrel
gammer	old woman
gill	ravine

hapt	wrapped
hind	farm worker
hoy	throw
keek	peep or pry
lanthorn	lantern
ling	heather
midden	refuse heap
moor	rough ground, usually heather-covered
nowt	nothing
peat hags	hummocks of peat
pipkin	small earthenware pot
posset	hot milk curdled with ale
press	cupboard
riving	tearing and tangling
sackless	stupid
sneck	latch or fastening
spate	flood
stop-work	hindrance
summat	something
tabor	small drum
taking	agitated state or excited condition
tatters	rags
trattles	tales or folk beliefs
tret	treat
trod	footpath

About the Author

Kathleen Hersom's first children's story was published in a national magazine while she was still in school. In the last thirteen years she has had seven books for young people published.

Before that she was a nursery school teacher in England, and in Holland and Germany was a civilian relief worker after World War II, mainly with children. When her own children grew up she worked voluntarily with mentally disabled children in a local hospital. This experience, combined with an interest in folklore, was the starting point for *The Half Child*.

Kathleen Hersom and her husband live in the village in which *The Half Child* begins and ends.